A CHRISTMAS SURPRISE

KIMBERLY ROSE JOHNSON

A Christmas Surprise
Published by Sweet Rose Press
U.S.A.

All Scripture quotations, unless otherwise indicated, are taken from the Holy Bible, New International Version®, NIV®. Copyright ©1973, 1978, 1984, 2011 by Biblica, Inc.™ Used by permission of Zondervan. All rights reserved worldwide. www.zondervan.com The "NIV" and "New International Version" are trademarks registered in the United States Patent and Trademark Office by Biblica, Inc.™

Dedication

This book is dedicated to my family and to everyone who encouraged me to not give up on my dream. Thank you for believing in me and my dream.

Acknowledgements

I am thrilled to be able to re-publish my first book I ever sold. This book will always hold a special place in my heart.

Special thanks to Aunt Nola, Uncle Bob, Aunt Jan and Uncle Milt for sharing Leavenworth with me and helping me see it through your eyes.

Finally, to my amazing critique partners, I thank you for all your suggestions and prayer support. So many people had a hand in making this book happen. You know who you are, and I thank you from the bottom of my heart.

To those of you who live in Leavenworth, please forgive my embellishments. I added things that don't exist and tweaked how buildings are set, all for the sake of the story. I hope you enjoy the result. Leavenworth is close to my heart, and I enjoy visiting as often as I am able.

1

Keira Noble peered out her apartment window at the first snow of the season, and a shiver ran through her. Snow set her on edge. Winter in the quaint Bavarian village of Leavenworth, Washington, always meant snow, but it was only the middle of October—much too early. Taking a sip of her morning coffee, she tucked her feet under her legs and snuggled deeper into the quilt. She closed her eyes, unwilling to gaze at the one thing that tortured her every winter.

"Momma." Four-and-a-half-year-old Cody padded out from his room and climbed into her lap. He nestled his head against her chest. "What's for breakfast?"

"How about oatmeal with blueberries?" She didn't open the candy shop until ten on weekdays, and treasured this time with her son.

"No."

"Really? I thought you loved blueberries."

He shook his head. "I like gummy worms. Can I have them in my oatmeal?"

"Eww. I don't think so." She gave him a squeeze and stood, setting him on the chaise. "Maybe after lunch you can pick out a few gummy worms from the bin." She smiled to herself, imagining he'd be the most popular kid in school someday with his access to candy.

She heard footsteps on the stairs that led to the alley. *Right on time.* Her best friend, Susan, had a way of showing up a couple of mornings a week for breakfast. She especially appreciated the visit today, considering the weather. Susan knew the fear snow brought on. Just the thought of driving now made her shudder. A rap on the door sounded and Keira flung the door open. "Morning." She gave Susan a quick hug and stepped back.

"Brrr. It's freezing out there." Susan unwound her scarf, pulled off her boots and hung her coat on a hook by the door. "Where's my little buddy?" She tiptoed over to the chaise. "Boo."

Cody squealed and laughed. "Aunt Susan, you always do that."

Sitting beside him, Susan wrapped an arm around Cody. "And you always laugh." She poked his belly. "What's for breakfast?"

"Oatmeal, but Mom said no gummy worms."

Susan snapped her fingers. "Bummer, but I'm sure she'll let us have brown sugar." Susan got up and walked into the kitchen. "I have a surprise for you."

Keira looked over her shoulder and raised a brow at her eccentric friend with the purple streaks in her long black hair. "I'm not a fan of surprises."

"You might like this one."

"Might?" She measured out the water and poured it into a saucepan. "I don't like the sound of this. Spill."

"Sorry." Susan pulled a card from her pocket. "Be at this address tonight at six and look hot."

"Huh?" Her friend had never told her to look hot. She turned around and took the card. "Visconti's?" She narrowed her eyes and crossed her arms. "What's going on? I'm not going to show up someplace unless I know why."

"Oh, all right. But you have to hear me out without interrupting."

"Su-san!"

"We set you up on a blind date." The words tumbled from her lips. "Pete is great. He's a veterinarian. Josh knows him from church and got to talking with him when he took his dog in the other day and realized the man has no social life—"

"And he immediately thought of me. I need to have a few words with your brother."

"You're interrupting."

"The two of you set me up? Why don't you go out with him?" It had to be an all-time low when her friends thought they needed to find her a man.

"He's not my type." Susan grinned and batted her lashes.

"Don't try that on me, missy." She'd date again when she was ready. "I'm not going." Keira turned her back on Susan and measured out the oats.

"But you have to. Josh already told him you'd be there."

"He will have to un-tell him. What kind of person agrees to a blind date at the last minute?"

"Actually, Pete's known about it for a week." She ducked her head. "I didn't know how to tell you, and then time got away from me and..." She shrugged. "You can't cancel now. It's too late."

Her friend knew her well. Of course she would've canceled. Keira bit her lip. Maybe it wouldn't hurt to meet the man. Besides, it would be rude to back out at the last minute, and she had always wanted to try the food at Visconti's, one of the best Italian restaurants around. Considering how small the village was, it was crazy she'd never been there before.

But there was one problem—Cody. Who would take care of her son and what would she tell him? Since her husband was killed four years ago in a car accident, she had gone out only once. Keira didn't want him to get confused or attached to a man who wasn't going to stick around. *Ack!* She was getting ahead of herself. It was only one date.

Susan touched her arm and lowered her voice. "You need this. It doesn't have to be anything serious, but it's time you started getting out there again. You keep yourself holed up in this apartment or the candy shop all the time. Live a little. And don't worry about Cody. I'll take care of him."

"Will you come here to watch him?"

Susan nodded. "Whatever you want."

An hour before closing Keira walked out of the back room and into the candy shop, the boxes in her arms partially blocking her view. Her chocolatier would be making a delivery soon and she needed to get these unpacked before her arrival.

"Whoa." Strong hands gripped her arms and kept her from colliding with the chest in front of her.

She peeked over the boxes and saw a man holding a charcoal-gray wool coat. "Oh, excuse me. I didn't hear you come in."

"No harm done." He flashed a smile.

Oh, but he was handsome—striking blue eyes, a strong chin and an incredible head of dark wavy hair on a fit body. She cleared her throat and stepped past him. What was she thinking? She had no business checking out the man. He was probably married anyway. "Are you here for the weekend?"

"No. I live in Leavenworth."

She pursed her lips. She really *did* need to get out more if Leavenworth had men like this. "Is there something I can help you find?" She set the boxes beside a display she'd been working on.

"I'd like a box of chocolates."

"That's our specialty," she said with a smile. "What kind?"

"I'm not sure. They're for my date, and I don't know what she likes. Maybe this is a mistake." He turned toward the door.

"Wait."

He turned back and raised a brow.

Keira stepped toward him. "Even if she doesn't like chocolate it's a nice gesture. And take it from a woman, most of us love chocolate. You can't go wrong with truffles."

"Are you sure? I don't want to look desperate."

Pete Harding sized up the petite woman clad in the traditional German costume some shopkeepers still wore. Her green eyes had a kindness about them. As if she really cared and wasn't just trying to make a sale. "Okay." A wide smile lit her face and he caught his breath. *Amazing.* He'd agreed to a blind date and regretted it all week, but felt guilty backing out. Now he was glad he hadn't, otherwise he wouldn't have come into the candy shop. Pete checked out the store clerk's left hand and didn't see a ring. Things were looking up. He didn't have much of a sweet tooth, but Christmas was fast approaching, and he hadn't done any shopping yet. Maybe this year he'd give everyone on his list a box of chocolates.

The woman held up two. "Which size would you like? I have a collection with six or a dozen."

No sense in overdoing it. Besides, he was more interested in the woman standing before him than his blind date. "Six."

"Good choice if you don't want to look desperate." She filled a gold-foil box with an assortment and rang up the purchase, thanking him for stopping in. Another customer with children came in, signaling it was time for him to leave. Too bad. He hadn't caught her name.

Keira looked in the mirror one last time. She'd spent more time than usual straightening her wavy hair with the flat iron. But now it hung perfectly straight and rounded to her chin. Black slacks and a red silk top completed the look. She tucked dangly silver earrings through her lobes and sighed. Was she really doing this? What would Michael think? She shook off the thought, suspecting her husband would've approved of her getting back out there.

A knock sounded on her bedroom door.

"Come in."

The door opened, and Susan walked in. "You look gorgeous! Pete isn't going to know what hit him."

"Are you sure? Maybe I should change." Her stomach flip-flopped. She didn't recall ever being this nervous before a date.

Susan reached out to her and grasped her arms. "No. You're perfect. And if you don't leave now you'll be really late. At least Visconti's is close."

Keira glanced at her watch. "I didn't realize the time. How will I know him?"

"Give the host or hostess your name, and don't worry. Pete has everything under control."

"Okay, if you say so." She liked a take-charge kind of man.

Susan grinned. "You'll be fine, Keira. Pete is a very nice man and even if it doesn't work out you'll get to know the town veterinarian and have a delicious meal."

"I don't own a pet, and I'm so nervous I don't think I can eat."

Susan waved her comment off. "Stop. Pete's great, and Cody's been asking for a puppy. Maybe he'll have a lead on a good choice."

Keira had no intention of getting her son a dog. There was no time to take care of a pet with all that needed to be done, running the candy shop and raising her boy.

Susan took a step closer and grabbed her hands. "Tonight will be fun. Just relax and live in the moment for a change." She briskly rubbed Keira's hands between her own. "You're freezing."

"That's because I'm terrified. Maybe I should just call the restaurant and leave a message that I'm ill. That's not far from the truth."

Susan took her by the shoulders and marched her to the door. "No way. I'll be watching from your living room window. It has a perfect view of Front Street, so don't even think about detouring and standing him up."

Keira's stomach fluttered. "I feel like a teen going on my first date." Why had she agreed to this? Cody smacked into her legs, wrapping his arms around them. Keira gently pried his arms loose and squatted down. "You be a good boy for Aunt Susan. Okay, Cody?"

He nodded. "Bring me back something?"

She chuckled. "We'll see." She slid into her wool coat, then blew a kiss to her two favorite people. "I won't be late."

Five steps down the stairs she nearly fell on the slippery surface. It wouldn't do to break a leg on the way there. She should've gone out through the store below, but old habits were hard to undo. She took the front way only if she was heading to work. She gripped the railing and continued down the snow-covered stairs with care. *Almost there.* Keira stepped onto the bottom step and her right foot slid forward on a patch of ice. A scream escaped her lips as her left knee buckled and she hit the sidewalk in a heap. She groaned and lay there for a second. *That didn't happen.* But her throbbing backside told a different story. She rolled over and stood. At least no one lingered about to see her graceful fall.

"Are you okay?" Susan called from the doorway. Keira stood and inspected her pants. Wet snow covered her legs. "I'm okay except for my pride, but I'd better change before I go. My pants are a mess." Instead of risking a repeat performance she went around to the storefront and unlocked the door. She climbed the interior stairs to her apartment.

The door swung open and Susan stood there with a panicked look on her face. "Are you sure you're okay?"

"No. Yes. What difference does it make?" Her pride stung and so did her hands, but she didn't have time to waste. What would she wear? This was her best outfit. She rushed to her bedroom with Susan close behind.

"Momma, why were you playing in the snow?"

"Cody, honey. I'm in a hurry. How about you build something with your blocks?"

"I want to play in the snow."

Keira sighed and squatted in front of him. "Tomorrow, okay? I'm meeting someone for dinner, and I'm late. Now scoot, so I can change." Her little guy padded into the front room and she zoomed for the dresser. Jeans would have to do. At least she had a nice pair that would go well with the blouse she already wore. She kicked off the slacks and slipped on the jeans. "Well?"

Susan nodded. "Very good. Now go." She nudged her toward the bedroom door. "And take the front. You don't have time to change again."

Keira passed Cody, who appeared to be building a fort out of blankets. "Bye. Love you."

"I know. Love you, too."

She smiled at her son's favorite phrase and closed the door. If Cody thought he knew everything at four, what would he be like at sixteen? But there was no time to worry about that now. A glance at her watch had her running through the candy store. She was never late. Of course Pete didn't know that. What a way to make a first impression. Oh, well, at least it was only ten past six. Surely he'd find it humorous once she explained. But what if he didn't?

Pete Harding nervously eyed the box of chocolates he'd

placed on the table. Maybe it was too much. Did men give chocolates on a blind date? It'd been forever since he'd last dated. He reached across the table to grab the box and tuck it back into his jacket pocket, but before he could a waiter approached. Pete pulled his hand back.

"Would you like to order something to drink. Dr. Harding?"

Pete glanced at his watch. "No thanks. I'm sure she'll be here any minute."

The waiter nodded and left just as his cell buzzed in his pocket. *Not tonight.* He knew that special sound. When he'd agreed to tonight's date he'd forgotten he was on call. "This is Dr. Harding." He listened as the answering service explained the emergency. "Okay. I'll be right there." He caught the waiter's eye and waited for him to approach. "I have to leave and my date isn't here yet. Would you let her know I had an emergency?" As much as he wanted to tell Keira himself, he couldn't wait. A dog's life depended on him.

He pushed back from the table and stood. Too bad he hadn't thought to ask for her phone number. He'd have to remember to call Josh ASAP and explain what happened. He strode for the stairs that led down to street level and past the beautiful blonde from the candy shop as she walked inside, completely oblivious to him. *Wow.* He slowed his gait. Gone was the German maiden costume and in its place a lovely modern woman in jeans that fit just right. He definitely would be buying candy for his family and friends this year.

Keira looked around the dining room as she followed the hostess and didn't see any males sitting alone. Her stomach flip-flopped. She'd committed one of the worst faux pas to her way of thinking—being late was rude and showed a lack of respect.

The young woman stopped at an empty table. "Dr. Harding was sitting in that spot, so I presume he intended this one for you." The hostess pulled out a chair for Keira.

"Thank you. Do you know where he went?"

She shook her head. "Sorry, no. He's probably in the restroom."

Keira thanked the hostess and sat. A small box that looked just like the ones she sold sat on the table in front of her. What a funny coincidence. Had her date been in the store recently? The man from that afternoon flashed in her mind, and she looked around. She recognized a few people and waved, but didn't see the man from earlier.

She picked up the menu and looked it over. A bowl of soup would be a good choice for her unsettled stomach. After placing the menu aside she glanced at the time. Maybe he'd gotten sick of waiting. But who would leave after only fifteen minutes? She'd stuck around for close to thirty minutes for people and never considered bailing. No, he had to be in the restroom like the hostess had suggested.

Keira sat back and tried to relax. White butcher paper covered a white tablecloth and draped gracefully. Crayons sat on the table. *How clever.* Maybe she should bring Cody here sometime. Her seat overlooked Front Street, and she could see her shop. A light shone in the window above with icicle lights hanging from the Bavarian-themed architecture. Tiny clear lights framed each window, reminding her of a storybook Christmas. If she didn't know better she'd say she was in the German Alps.

A waiter approached her table.

"Have you seen the man who was sitting here?"

"I'm sorry. I don't know. I just took over for the waiter who had this table. Would you like to order now?"

"Not yet." She checked the time again—six-thirty. Maybe he had left. But it didn't make sense. Why go to all this trouble only to leave? One thing was certain. She couldn't go home now. It would be too humiliating to admit she'd been stood up. Well not technically, but it felt like it just the same. She waved to the waiter. "I'd like to order a bowl of your minestrone, please."

Keira stared out the window at the falling snowflakes. How could something so beautiful cause nightmares? Just once she'd like to see snow and not feel like burying her head under a blanket until spring. She sighed and returned her gaze to her surroundings. Somehow the elegant setting fit in with the loft vibe the room projected. Michael would've hated this place. He was more of a fast-food kind of guy, but in spite of being alone she liked it very much. Too bad Pete had deserted her.

The waiter placed a bowl of soup in front of her. "Can I get you anything else?"

She shook her head. "No, thanks."

The soup warmed her all the way down. But the idea of answering Susan's questions made her shiver inside. Her friend would want details, and she didn't care to share. Had her date taken one look at her on his way back from the restroom and slipped out? Maybe she wasn't attractive anymore. Keira's cheeks flamed and she pushed the bowl aside. This was all too humiliating. Her first date since forever, and he'd cut out on her.

She picked up the box of chocolates he'd left behind and opened the lid. Her eyes widened. These looked exactly like the box she'd put together for the handsome man this afternoon, but he didn't seem the type to stand up his date. Besides, he didn't indicate it was a blind date. She replaced the lid and tucked the candy into her coat pocket. She'd give them to Susan for watching Cody.

The soup really did smell wonderful and she couldn't resist. Date or no date, there was no way she could leave the nearly full bowl behind. She spooned the delightful flavors into her mouth. "Mmm." There was nothing like comfort food on a snowy night.

After paying, she went down the stairs and outside. A small crew of two worked at putting Christmas decorations on the unadorned structures. Soon all the trees would be covered in lights along with the lovely buildings. She tucked hands into her pockets and picked her way across the street. She'd go in the front door. No sense in risking the exterior stairs.

Leavenworth knew how to do Christmas. In a month

or so the village would be shoulder-to-shoulder people every weekend. The Lighting Festival drew tourists to the town in droves. In the past she'd been so swamped at the candy shop during the day, she missed all the excitement outside. But at night she'd close up the store and watch the festivities from her apartment window. This year Cody had asked to join in the fun. She'd have to hurry up and find a temporary worker so her son could experience Leavenworth at its best.

Keira unlocked the store, kicked snow off her boots and stepped inside, locking up before tiptoeing upstairs. It was only seven, but if Cody was asleep, she didn't want to wake him. She opened the door slowly and spotted her son on the chaise with Susan, who held his favorite book on her lap. Cody's eyes drooped closed and his little cheeks were flushed.

Keira walked over to the duo and squatted. "How was Cody?" she asked softly.

"Just fine. You're back early." She frowned. "Didn't it go well?"

Keira hesitated. "The restaurant was very nice."

"What else? Tell me everything and don't leave out any details."

Keira grimaced at her friend's persistence. "I had a delicious bowl of minestrone, and the setting was neat. I think I might even take Cody there sometime. They had butcher paper covering the tablecloths and there were crayons for the children to color on the table."

"He would love that." Susan set the book aside. "You

want help putting him to bed?"

"No, thanks. I'll just carry him. Be right back, don't leave." Keira tucked Cody into her arms and stood.

"Momma, you're home."

"Shh. I love you, precious, now go back to sleep."

Cody snuggled into the crook of her neck and closed his eyes.

Keira laid him between the sheets and pulled the covers to his chin. She rested her hand on his cheek and gave him a kiss. Seeing her son sleeping peacefully made the crazy times less stressful.

She tiptoed from the room and left the door slightly ajar. Cody had a night-light, but he didn't like his door closed.

Susan stood when she came back into the family room. "Since you're back so early, I take it you and Pete didn't hit it off."

"You could say that." She pulled the box of truffles from her coat pocket. "Here, I don't need these and thought you'd enjoy them."

"He bought you chocolates! That's so sweet." She grinned. "No pun intended. Why don't you keep them?"

Keira giggled. "Sweetie, I own a candy store. Take the truffles. You'll love them."

Susan grinned. "Thanks. Cody was great. We played fort, then he had a bath and was a little angel."

"I'm glad. Thanks for watching him."

"Hey, it was the least I could do. Sorry it didn't go like I'd hoped."

"No worries." Keira walked Susan to the door and waited while her friend slipped on some rubber-and-metal traction things over her boots. "Will I see you tomorrow?"

"Doubtful. I have a ton of work to do, but I'll be by for breakfast on Sunday." Susan gave her a hug and stepped down the stairs with no problem.

Keira watched with envy. She needed to get a pair of those boot chains for herself. If she'd had those tonight her evening would have gone much differently. She sighed and closed the door. No more dating for her. From now on she'd focus on her son and her business.

Pete finished the last suture and breathed a little easier. It looked like the Australian shepherd would make it, barring any complications. "Go ahead and finish up. I'll stick around here tonight to watch our patient."

Meghan, his assistant of six months, nodded and began cleaning.

Now to call Josh. He glanced at the wall clock and cringed—nine o'clock already.

"Anything wrong?" Meghan asked.

"No, I just need to make a call before it gets too late."

She reached with gloved hands for the surgical instruments. "Hot date tonight?"

"Something like that."

A short time later he locked up behind Meghan and hustled for the phone. He punched in Josh's number and waited. After seven rings Josh finally picked up.

"This'd better be important," the voice growled.

"Josh, it's Pete."

"Oh, hey." His gravelly voice cleared. "How'd it go tonight? Must've gone well if you're calling so late."

"It's only nine-thirty, and no, it didn't go well at all." He explained what had happened. "I'd like to call her and apologize, but I don't have her number, or her last name, so I couldn't even look her up."

Josh gave him the information. "'Night."

Pete reached for the phone again and thought better of it. If she was early to bed like Josh, he didn't want to risk waking her. He'd call tomorrow and explain. In the meantime he had a patient to take care of. He let his mind wander to the woman from the candy shop. Maybe he'd stop in there again tomorrow. It was never too early to tackle his Christmas list. Well, maybe October was a bit early, but he could pick up a box of chocolates for the clinic.

2

Saturday morning Keira rushed through her apartment, following the sound of the ringing phone. *Where could it be?* Standing still, she listened for the next ring and headed for the kitchen. Locating the phone, she checked the caller ID and didn't recognize the number. Instead of answering, she took the phone to her room, placed it on the charger and continued making her bed. Whoever it was could leave a voice mail.

Cody would be awake soon, and there'd be no peace, thanks to his energy. If only she had the kind of pep her son did. Keira's mother-in-law would be by to get Cody at nine-thirty for their weekly day together. Cody loved Saturdays with his grandma. Keira liked them because she didn't need to keep an eye on the back room where her son usually played. Good thing, too, because Saturdays were generally the busiest day of the week. Now that the holidays were approaching she'd be even busier. She really needed to hire a seasonal helper. Susan might know a responsible teen looking to earn a little Christmas money.

"Hi, Momma." Cody padded into the room, rubbing his eyes, and climbed onto her freshly made bed.

"Good morning. Did you sleep well?"

He nodded, crawled to the head of the bed and snuggled into the decorative pillows.

"Grandma Noble will be here soon. The cereal is on the table. Please eat breakfast and then get dressed. Don't forget to brush your teeth."

Cody pushed up and slid off the bed. "Honey Nut Cheerios?"

"Of course. Hurry up now." Keira tried to keep a straight face. She didn't have time to play this morning.

Her son nodded and sprinted from the room.

Keira followed, but more slowly.

"Who called. Momma?"

"I don't know. I forgot to see if there's a message. Eat up while I check." She scooted to the bedroom. Sure enough, there was one. A moment later she heard the sound of a man's voice.

"Hi, Keira. I'm sorry about last night. I had an emergency at the clinic and had to leave. I assume you were just running late and didn't stand me up." He chuckled. "Anyway, I hope you enjoyed the chocolates. Maybe we can try again sometime. Give me a call." He left his number.

She plopped down onto the edge of the bed. It would have been so much easier if he hadn't asked her to call, but there was no sense in prolonging the inevitable. She punched in his number and waited. He picked up on the second ring. "Is this Pete?"

"Yes. Keira?"

"I got your message, and thanks for the candy. I'm sorry it didn't work out last night, but I don't think it's a good idea to try again."

"I understand. No problem." He sounded relieved and ended the call.

She stared at the phone in disbelief. It seemed like neither of them wanted the date. Keira giggled and felt happy for the first time since the snow had started. What a relief to have that taken care of. Dating was too much pressure, especially a blind date. She never should've agreed to it in the first place. Not that Susan had given her much choice.

Pete pumped a fist in the air and spun around to see his assistant standing in the doorway to his office with raised brows and a hint of a smile on her face. "Meghan, I didn't know you were there."

"Obviously. I take it that was good news." She pushed her long mocha-colored hair back over her ears and rested a hand in the front pocket of her jeans.

Although attractive, he'd never felt any special connection with this woman. However, her skills as a veterinary assistant were impeccable, so he put up with her nosiness. He cleared his throat. "Yes." Too bad he hadn't closed the door and avoided her questioning look. "I'm going to phone Lady's owner and have her come in. Lady's doing well and is ready to go home."

"Great. Looks like you have everything under

control." Meghan held up a purple scarf. "I forgot this last night. See you Monday."

His assistant left without a backward glance. He sank into the high-back leather desk chair. Time to get down to business and release his patient.

Keira handed a dark chocolate-covered almond sample to a customer and watched the woman's eyes light up with pleasure. Keira grinned at the true chocolate lover. Maybe she should entice her with a praline. Before she could, the door opened and the handsome man from yesterday walked in. His dark wavy hair kissed his eyebrows, and his strong shoulders filled out the black Henley shirt that hugged his chest just right. Keira pulled her attention back to the woman she was helping and finished filling an assorted half-pound box for her.

Keira smiled at the waiting man. "I'll be with you as soon as I finish up here."

"No problem."

She quickly completed the box and collected payment, then turned to the first man that had piqued her interest since her husband's death. "You're back. Were the truffles a hit?"

He frowned. "She thanked me for them, but to be honest the night was a disaster. I was called away on an emergency before she ever arrived."

What was the chance that this man and her date were the same person? All the evidence pointed in that direction. Should she say something?

"I was hoping you could help me with my Christmas shopping."

She laughed. "So soon?"

He looked at her with confusion on his face. Of course he didn't understand the relevance of her statement. How could he? "My chocolates won't keep longer than a week. The bin candy will keep, if you'd like that." She leaned closer and lowered her voice. "They're good, too, but honestly don't compare to the freshly made ones."

His brow furrowed. "No. I was hoping for the special chocolates." He looked around the store and picked up a teddy bear holding a bouquet of packaged candy. "My niece might like this." He brought it to the counter.

"She probably would. If you'd like, I could write up your order and have it wrapped and ready to go for you the week of Christmas. I also ship if you'd prefer."

His gaze met hers. She caught her breath as his blue eyes crinkled at the edges. Where had this man been hiding?

"That's a great idea." He pulled a small piece of paper from his pocket. "I'd like to get a one-pound assorted box for everyone on my list, and a box to take with me today."

Keira felt her eyes widen. His list had ten people on it! "Wonderful." She proceeded to write down his information. "Do you want to pick up the boxes or ship them?"

He thought for a moment. "I'll ship all but two. I'd

like a box for the clinic, and I'll pick the other one up just before Christmas."

"Clinic? Are you a doctor?"

"Veterinarian."

"It is you!"

"Pardon me?"

She held out her hand. "I'm Keira. We were supposed to have a date last night, but thanks to the snow and my clumsiness you were gone before I arrived."

He took her hand and gave it a warm squeeze. "I'm really sorry I missed you. I saw you come in, but didn't realize you were my date. Josh didn't tell me anything about you."

"And you still agreed to meet me? You're a daring man." He chuckled. "Well, Josh is a good guy. I trust his judgment."

Oh, she liked this man. Her cheeks warmed at the interest she saw, and she ducked her head. Her heart beat a rapid staccato. Whew. It was hot in here.

"I don't suppose you'd consider coffee with me?"

"I'd like that, but I'm the only one here." Today would be out altogether. Her mother-in-law always brought Cody back at six o'clock when the store closed.

"Your boss runs a tight ship. You'd think on a Saturday there'd be extra help."

"Yeah, well, the boss has been busy."

He shifted his stance. "How long have you been working here?"

"Six years."

"Wow. That's a long time." He handed her his debit card.

"Sure is." She ran his card, then gave it back to him. She handed him several Christmas cards that were left over from last year, similar to the kind florist shops carried. "Go ahead and write your messages on the cards, and I'll make sure they're attached to the boxes."

He took a pen from the cup on the counter and scribbled out several messages. "Since you're not available today, how about lunch tomorrow? I'm free after church." He looked expectant, then a shadow of uncertainty clouded his eyes. "Or coffee if you'd prefer."

"I don't know. Sundays are pretty busy here." She had to come up with some time that would work, or he'd think she wasn't interested. "I really would like to get to know you, Pete, but running the store eats up a lot of my time."

"I didn't realize you're the manager."

"Actually I own the place. It was my late husband's dream to have a candy shop." She shrugged. "It meets my needs, and I've grown attached to the people here in Leavenworth."

"I'm sorry for your loss."

"Thanks." Now she'd done it. Why had she mentioned Michael? She just assumed Josh had filled him in on the basics of her life, but apparently he hadn't. The door opened and several people loaded down with bags stomped in. Why couldn't they kick the snow off outside? Oh, well, that's what the rug was for. "I'm sorry, Pete, I need—" She motioned toward the customers with her eyes.

"Of course. I'll let you get back to work." He handed her the cards. "It was good talking with you." He strode to the door and turned and grinned before exiting.

Keira's heart stuttered. Somehow she'd have to find a way to escape this place for a few hours. She smiled and took a deep breath, willing her pulse to slow. No man had ever affected her like this. She'd loved Michael, but it hadn't been the same with him. They'd been the best of friends and had known each other since high school.

They'd had an ease about their relationship, somewhat like the comfy feel of a favorite pair of jeans. But Pete was different.

Sunday afternoon Pete sat in his favorite easy chair and watched the flames dance in the river-rock fireplace. He glanced toward the rustic wood clock hanging over the mantel in his old farmhouse. He planned to fix the place up one room at a time, but so far hadn't touched a thing besides replacing the old mantel. The house had good bones and deserved to be restored.

Restoration seemed to be a theme in his life. A pang of regret pierced him like a direct hit from a missile. Unfortunately some things couldn't be fixed.

The phone jarred him from his thoughts. A quick glance at the caller ID put a smile on his face. "Keira." Since he'd seen her last, he couldn't get her image out of his mind. She had a delicate mouth and nose, and her straight blond hair draped down to a perfectly rounded chin. But what grabbed him the most was her clear green eyes.

"Hi there. I did the impossible and found a part-time helper. If you'd still like to grab coffee, I can get away for about thirty minutes. I'm training her today, but I think she can handle being on her own for a short time."

A half hour wasn't long, but he'd take what he could get. "Sure. When?"

"Does two o'clock work for you? You could meet me at my store."

"I'll be there." The day was turning out better than expected. He'd let the fire die out, then head into town.

Keira walked her new hire through a sale and her shoulders relaxed. Holly was good at the register and, because she'd been a customer since she was a young teen, she knew the product well. How fortunate that Susan recommended her. The best thing was. Holly attended nursing

school in Wenatchee and only wanted part-time work so she'd have time for classes and studying.

"I'm going to step out for coffee at two. Do you think you'll be okay?"

Holly bit her bottom lip and unease covered her face. "I don't know. I'm a little nervous. What if I have a problem?"

"I'll leave you my cell number." Hopefully her short time with Pete would go well. The timing couldn't be better since her son was off with his grandma again. All in all everything had worked out better than she'd expected. It had stopped snowing, and the sun shone bright in the blue sky. This was her favorite kind of day. Snow was still on the ground, but it didn't seem so bad with the sun shining.

She hummed her favorite tune, ignoring the piano music piping through the speakers mounted on the wall.

Holly cast a glance her way. "Christmas already. Seriously?"

"It's my happy song." Keira shrugged. Pete had put Christmas front and center in her mind, and she couldn't help herself.

Holly raised her hands and shook her head. "No problem. Just surprised. I suppose if you can't hum Christmas music in October in Leavenworth, where can you?"

"Exactly. After all, this village wasn't voted the best place to spend Christmas for nothing. We know how to do the holiday right."

The bells on the door jangled as it opened and a burst of cold air rushed in along with Pete. Was it two already? She glanced at her watch. Where had the time gone? "Hi, Pete. Just give me a second." She turned to Holly. "My cell number is by the register. I won't be long."

Holly gave her a tight smile. "Okay."

Keira grabbed her jacket and strolled to the door

where Pete waited. "I hope there isn't a line. I really can't be gone long." She kept her voice low so Holly wouldn't hear. No need for Holly to think she was worried.

Pete held the door for her and offered his arm. "The sidewalks are clear, but the street's a little slick."

She slipped her hand into the crook of his arm. This felt so weird. She barely knew the man and here she was hanging on to him. But he was right, the street was slick. Her brow scrunched. Maybe this had been a bad idea. She needed to focus on Cody and the shop, not dating. But since Cody was off with his grandma, her son would be none the wiser if things didn't work out with Pete.

"You okay?" Pete looked down at her with concern in his eyes.

"I'm...fine. Just a little nervous. Snow isn't my favorite thing. It's good we're walking because I don't drive on slippery roads." Her foot slid, and she gripped his arm tighter.

"Careful. I don't want you to break something."

"No kidding." She held tight until they crossed the road, then let go. "I'm not sure how I'd work with a broken arm or leg."

"Me neither, come to think of it. Can you imagine trying to do surgery on crutches or with only one hand?"

Keira laughed. "Or tie a bow around a box of chocolates."

They walked up the stairs and into the coffee shop. The strong scent of java enveloped her. Keira slid out of her jacket. "It's hot in here."

He took off his gloves and they stood side by side in line. "What would you like?"

"A tall mocha."

"Sounds good." Pete ordered and paid. He guided them to a little table by a window. The space was tight, but the whole store was on the small side. "I'm glad it worked out to get together. I'm really sorry to have run out on you like I did the other night."

"No worries. How's the dog?"

"Doing well."

Conversation flowed freely for the next fifteen minutes or so. Keira couldn't stop smiling, her cheeks felt warm, and she knew it wasn't from the heat. Pete was a cool guy. "What brought you to Leavenworth?"

"A job. I've always loved this area and when a position opened at the clinic I jumped at it. It's hard to beat this place as far as I'm concerned. There's plenty of snow in the winter for skiing and snowmobiling, and great hiking, fishing and rafting the rest of the year."

"Seattle is close to all of that."

"Sure, but I was sick of the rain and concrete jungle. This is much more to my liking. I only have to step outside my front door to enjoy nature."

She wrinkled her nose. How could anyone prefer snow to the safer roads on the other side of the pass?

"I take it you don't agree?"

She shook her head.

"Why do you stay? You could sell your shop and start over somewhere else, or even close for the winter and live someplace warm. However, I must warn you, even though we just met. I'd be sad to see you leave."

"Thanks. But don't worry. I could never do that. My friends are here, and I enjoy the candy shop and my customers. Starting over someplace else would be so difficult, especially with the economy the way it is. Besides, this is home, and Cody is close to family here. His grandparents live in town, and I want him to know his family."

"Cody?"

"My son. He's a four-and-a-half-year-old bundle of energy." She smiled and looked down at her cup, warmth filling her. She had an adorable son and now a man who might open her heart to new possibilities. She raised her eyes just as he looked away, but the expression that crossed his face lanced the joy that had started to fill the dry places inside her. Anger or regret. It passed so swiftly she couldn't decipher which. "What's wrong?"

"Nothing." He stood. "You should probably get back. It's already two forty-five."

Keira caught her breath, shocked at how quickly the time had passed. "I promised Holly I'd only be gone half an hour." She jumped up and slipped into her jacket, then tossed her cup in the receptacle.

Pete stayed silent as they hustled up the street. He stopped just outside the candy store. "Look, I know this was my idea, but I don't think things will work out between us."

Shocked, Keira blurted out, "Why not?" before she

could stop herself.

"It's not you, it's me. I don't date women with kids."

"What?" How absurd. But she would never have a relationship with a man who couldn't accept and love her son as his own, so it was better to find out now before her heart was involved. Who was she kidding? She'd fallen for Pete the instant he'd walked into her shop.

"It's a long story. Here's the shortened version—I was in a relationship with a single mother for several years. I expected to marry her and loved her son as my own. But she had another plan. She left me, and I haven't seen either of them since."

Keira's heart softened. He'd clearly been wounded by this woman. "I'm really sorry you went through that, Pete. Not all women will break your trust like that." She glanced into the shop, then back at him. "Thanks for your honesty and for the coffee. Bye, Pete." She brushed past him and went inside.

Pete's chest ached. The disappointment and pity on Keira's face stung. This couldn't be happening. Josh had never mentioned Keira's son. But then, he hadn't mentioned she was a widow, either. Pete frowned. If he'd known he never would've allowed himself to be attracted to her, but now it was too late. They'd connected on a level he hadn't expected and in a very short time. For the first time since Becky had destroyed his trust, his heart had connected with a woman. It was as if he and Keira had known each other forever. He tucked his hands in his coat pockets and hunched over.

He couldn't get involved with another woman who had a child. He still missed little Jack. They'd been the best of buddies. The kid had followed him everywhere and had even started calling him "Dad." He would've been "Dad," too, if Becky hadn't cheated on him and taken off with another man.

No, he couldn't go there. It was one thing to have his own child, no one could take him away, but if he grew close to Keira and her son and things didn't work out, it would be like losing Jack all over again. His heart couldn't take it—not a second time. And Keira needed to consider her son, too. It wasn't only adults who could get hurt when things didn't work out.

He quickened his pace. His musings served no purpose except to remind him to guard his heart. Besides, he much preferred animals to people these days. At least they were faithful. He never should've allowed Josh to talk him into meeting Keira. The hurt and disappointment he saw in her eyes still stung. She didn't want anything to do with him and with good reason. He turned and looked back toward the candy shop.

3

Four weeks later

Two days before Thanksgiving, business picked up. Thankfully customers were snapping up Keira's fresh chocolates in droves, which in turn eased the congestion in the storage room since that's where the decorative boxes were stored. Soon there'd be room for Cody's cot again. She locked up the shop. "Come on, Cody. Let's head home."

Cody bounded from the back room. "I made a castle out of one of the boxes. Momma."

"Very nice." She took his hand and they climbed the stairs together. Susan would be joining them for dinner soon, and she needed to stick the frozen pizzas in the oven. No one ever accused her of being a culinary success although she made a mean lasagna. Michael had always been the cook. She sighed.

"What's wrong. Mom?"

"I'm just tired."

"Not me." Cody opened the door to their apartment and clicked on *Clifford the Big Red Dog,* his favorite cartoon.

Keira turned on the oven and pulled two pizzas from the freezer. She laid them on the counter and gave them a dubious look. She wouldn't be winning the Best Parent award tonight. She shrugged and placed them in the oven.

The doorbell rang and Cody hollered, "I'll get it." She heard his feet scamper toward the entryway.

She leaned out of the kitchen. "Make sure it's Aunt Susan before you open the door."

Susan breezed in, loaded down with a large bowl and a canvas bag. "How are my two favorite people?"

Cody hugged her leg and then charged back to the TV. Susan placed the bowl and bag on the counter. "I brought salad and dessert."

"You didn't have to do that." But she was already pulling the cellophane off the salad.

"Yes, I did. I love my greens." She beamed a cheesy grin. "What's going on with Pete?"

Keira's hands stilled over the silverware drawer, and then she slowly pulled out three forks. She cleared her throat. "Um, nothing." She'd actually seen him several times around town and at church over the past few weeks. He had been polite, and they'd even struck up a friendship of sorts, but it was clear the man guarded his heart. Not that she blamed him. It was hard to let go of the past. She of all people understood that.

Susan crossed her arms. "Okay, what gives?"

Keira brushed past her to set the small kitchen table.

"Nothing, but Pete is history, at least in the romantic sense. I really like him, but there's something major standing in the way." She set the forks on the table, giving herself time to answer. She smoothed her hands against her jeans and took a breath before she turned. "Pete doesn't date women with kids."

"What? I can't believe you didn't mention this sooner. You've known him, what, a month? When were you planning to tell me this?" Susan stopped, one hand on the refrigerator door, the other holding half a pumpkin cheesecake. She narrowed her eyes. "I saw you two talking last week at church. You appeared friendly."

"Yes, we're friendly, but I didn't see any reason to bring up the no-kid thing. I guess I just didn't want to talk about it. It hurt. Besides, I *knew* you'd ask questions." She gave Susan a pointed look and sighed. "It's not like we were seeing each other or anything. We had coffee only once. We talk at church. But we're *not* dating." Keira shrugged, keeping an eye toward the family room to make sure Cody was still engrossed in his program.

Susan's jaw dropped open, and she quickly snapped it shut. "Oh, sweetie. I'm so sorry. I had no idea. When I saw the two of you together, I just thought...you looked so... Never mind. Consider the subject dropped."

"Thanks." Keira added napkins to the table setting and changed the subject. "I got the most interesting invite in the mail today for a Christmas Surprise Ball. Did you get one?"

Susan nodded. "Yes. Are you going?"

"I'm considering it. Cody would have fun. What about you?"

Susan shrugged. "Not really my kind of thing, but I don't know."

"Yeah. You know how I hate surprises—and I'd have to get a dress."

Susan nodded. "I asked around, but no one seems to know what the surprise part is all about, or even who the sponsor is."

"Odd." She imagined what a ball would have looked like a hundred years ago and sighed. "It does sound exciting. But I don't know."

"You should go. Like you said, Cody would have fun. I can't wait until next weekend when he sees the Christmas Lighting Festival."

Keira grinned. "We'll see, but I'm kind of looking forward to the festival, too. I haven't been since Cody was born." She had so many things she wanted to do in Leavenworth.

"Will you be going to your in-laws' house for Thanksgiving?"

"Yes. I'm bringing the dessert." Hopefully the weather would cooperate. "You know what really stinks?" Keira set the table for three.

"Hmm?"

"I like him. I'd actually started fantasizing about a future with him. We seemed so right for each other." She pulled the pizzas from the oven and grabbed the pizza cutter.

"Are we talking about Pete?"

Keira paused, holding the cutting wheel midair. "I know I need to forget about him in the romantic sense, but he's kind of stuck on my brain, especially since I've been running into him so often."

Susan put tongs in the salad and placed it on the table. "Maybe you should start dating. I don't mean another blind date, either. Don't you know any single men?"

"Probably." She loved her friend, but she'd seriously gone loony with that suggestion. She leaned into the family room. "Dinner's ready, Cody. Please turn off the TV."

Cody obeyed and scampered to the table. The three sat, and Keira offered a blessing. A lively conversation about *Clifford* ensued and the pizza was demolished in no time. To Keira's chagrin she'd eaten at least half a pizza on her own. She couldn't help it. Angst made her crave carbs, and pizza was the perfect fix. At least Susan didn't bring up dating in front of Cody.

Later that evening Susan whispered in her ear as she pulled on her coat, "I'm going to find the perfect man for you if it's the last thing I do."

Keira gave her friend a squeeze and ignored the promise. "Will you come with me and Cody to the festival next Friday?"

"Sure. Sounds like fun. See you Sunday, and if I don't see you sooner, have a nice Thanksgiving."

"You, too." Keira locked up behind Susan and pondered her friend's advice. Was dating a good idea? She hadn't even considered it until recently and that hadn't worked out well. But in spite of her busy life she was lonely and longed for companionship. Hmm, maybe she should get a dog. She chuckled. It'd be just her luck to end up with a sick dog and have to take him to see Pete.

Cody padded over to her. "What's so funny. Momma?"

"Just thinking about getting a dog," she mumbled.

"Really?" His face lit with excitement. "I want a dog like Clifford."

Oh, boy. She'd done it now. Why had she voiced that thought? "I don't know, Cody. A dog is a lot of work, and I'm pretty busy. Plus, an animal that big would never fit through the door, and we don't have a yard to keep him in." She didn't have the heart to tell him *Clifford* dogs weren't real. In his young mind, *Clifford the Big Red Dog* was as real as he was.

"I'll take care of him. I promise."

Keira ruffled his hair with her hand and smiled. Those soulful blue eyes of his never failed to get her. It was like looking straight into his daddy's gaze. How could she deny this boy a puppy? She hadn't started Christmas shopping yet, and Cody never asked for much. But a dog? "How about you go brush your teeth and get ready for bed?"

"Aww, Mom. I'm never going to get a dog." He shuffled away, taking a piece of her heart with him. How did kids do that?

The Christmas ball invitation and ticket on the

counter caught her attention. She picked it up again and read the small print at the bottom: No Children Allowed. There went that idea, but some part of her ached to dress up and forget chocolates and customers.

Pete handed a canvas bag containing four bottles of sparkling cider to Josh. "Happy Thanksgiving."

"Hey, glad you made it." Josh took the bag and closed the door behind Pete. "When you said you were on call today we were afraid you wouldn't show."

"So far so good. There were a few minor issues this morning, but this afternoon has been quiet. I imagine I'll be busy fielding emergency calls later when people feed their pets leftovers that make them sick."

"Let's hope not. Come on into the family room. The kids and I are watching the game."

Pete slipped out of his jacket and hung it on the coatrack by the entrance. "My kind of family—football and good food."

Josh chuckled and led the way.

The rest of the day went by in a blur with laughter and too much to eat. His thoughts drifted to Keira. He'd gotten to know her a little over the past month, and she didn't seem like the kind of woman who'd cheat on him and then take off. But then again, neither had Becky. No, he'd made the right decision in breaking things off with her before anything started. Kids just complicated things. It was the best thing for her son, too. What if he got close to Keira's son and he and Keira later broke up? The child could be hurt. There was just too much risk for everyone.

Josh's oldest son, Trent, stood tall with his shoulders back. "You want to play a game of checkers? My dad says I'm a worthy opponent, whatever that means." A bashful smile settled on his lips.

Pete glanced toward Josh, who winked. "Why not? Set it up. But after that I need to head out." He followed Trent to the card table Josh had placed in the bay window. He hadn't played checkers since grade school, but surely he could hold his own against a nine-year-old. "Do you want to go first?"

"Sure." Trent set up the red pieces, while Pete placed the black ones on the correct squares. Trent slid a piece forward and Pete followed by doing the same with his.

Several plays later Pete realized he'd been had. This kid was a checker shark. The game was over before it began. "How did you get so good at this?"

"When I was little I got sick a lot. My mom and dad played checkers with me."

Pete looked to Josh for an explanation, but Josh had left the room.

Trent jumped the last of his kings. "I win!"

"You sure did." He watched the boy a second. Would it bother him if he asked? But then again, Trent had brought the subject up. "You never said why you were sick all the time."

"I'm allergic to cats, and Mom and Dad didn't know. My friend has a cat, so I can't play at his house anymore."

"I see. Cat allergies can be bad. Good thing they figured out the problem."

Trent nodded. "I actually ended up with pneumonia once because I kept getting sicker and sicker."

"Well, I'm glad you're fine now."

"Me, too." Trent grinned wide. "And the best part is I'm an expert checker player."

Pete chuckled. "That you are." He stretched and patted his stomach. "I better head out before I'm tempted to eat more of your mom's delicious apple pie and need to be rolled out the door."

Trent giggled and stood. "Dad! Pete's leaving."

Josh sauntered back into the room with a plate covered in tinfoil. "Leftovers. Laura insisted."

"Sounds good to me." There was nothing like leftover turkey and dressing. "I hope she included a piece of pie."

"Of course." Josh followed him to the door. "Before you go, my sister Susan asked about a dog. Keira is looking for a small dog for her son."

Pete shrugged into his jacket, wishing he could ask how she was really doing. Sure, he saw her around town and at church, and she was always friendly, but he didn't like to think that he'd hurt her. He'd closed the door on a relationship, though, so maybe it was better not to ask. Might give Josh the wrong idea. "I'll keep my ears open. Do they have a particular breed in mind?"

Josh chuckled. "Susan said Cody wants a dog like Clifford."

"The cartoon?"

Josh laughed outright. "One and the same."

Pete grinned. "Don't think that'll work, but I'll give Keira a call if I come across any small-to-medium breeds in need of a home." Suddenly an idea percolated, and he couldn't wait to find a dog for Keira's son.

A week after Thanksgiving, Pete drove home from work, his fingers gripping the steering wheel. The recent snow had iced over, making driving treacherous. He had studded tires but decided to take it easy. Something on the side of the road grabbed his attention. He glanced out the driver's-side window and frowned. He pulled off the road and stepped out. The SUV hummed quietly in the still air. He shuffled across the road and spoke softly to the small bundle of brown-and-blond fur. "Hey, there." He stood still and waited for the dog to respond.

The beagle whimpered and limped toward him. Pete reached down and cradled her in his arms. "You're such a sweet girl. What are you doing out here in the cold?" He took the animal to his Toyota 4Runner, rubbing his fingers along the fur where a collar should have been. Pete always kept a blanket in the backseat and spread it out before placing the dog on it. He'd take the beagle to the clinic and check her out. She favored her left paw, but he'd know more when he got her on the exam table.

Other than a dirty coat and the paw, the animal seemed well cared for. He made a U-turn and headed back toward town. He'd check for a microchip. It'd be best to locate the owners tonight. He'd hate to leave her at the

43

animal shelter.

A few minutes later he pulled back into his assigned spot at the clinic. The beagle buried her head in his elbow as he carried her inside. He felt her start to relax and she snuggled into his arms like she belonged there.

"You're back!" Meghan stood from her desk chair. Her eyebrows rose. "Well, who do you have there?"

"I found her alongside Highway 2." He took the dog into one of the rooms and placed her on an exam table. "Now let's see that paw." Lifting her front left leg, he examined her pads closely. Sure enough a small sliver of glass was stuck in her paw. "How did you find glass with the ground covered in snow?" He ran his hands along her sides to check for any abnormalities. Everything felt fine.

Meghan popped into the room. "Need anything?"

He rattled off a few items and took the dog's temperature while waiting for his assistant to return.

"Here we are." Meghan brought in a tray with the supplies and placed them on the counter.

"Please stay. I might need you." In no time Pete removed the glass. Thankfully the paw was not infected and didn't require wrapping. "Blondie needs a bath, but first let's see if she has a microchip. I'd like to let her owners know she's safe."

Meghan smirked. "Blondie? I thought she didn't have a tag."

He chuckled. "I dubbed her that because of her tan ears." He scratched Blondie behind the ears and spoke softly to her. "She's a beauty, don't you think?"

"A little dirty, but that can be fixed."

Pete picked up the animal and passed her off to Meghan, but couldn't help giving the dog another scratch behind the ears. Her brown eyes stared up into his. "Let me know what you find out."

"Will do. You need a Blondie of your own. I've never seen you take to a dog like this. You're usually all business."

"Not true. I treat all my patients the same." A smile teased his lips. Okay, so maybe Blondie touched his heart a little more than most.

"Whatever you say." Meghan took Blondie from the room.

Meghan's words played in his head again and sent his mind tumbling toward the woman who had consumed his thoughts since the day they'd met, no matter how hard he tried not to think about her. He'd certainly taken to Keira right from the start.

Pete went to his office and waited. What would he do if the dog didn't have a chip? Sending her to the animal shelter didn't appeal. He thought of Cody and shook his head. There was no sense getting ahead of himself. A knock sounded on his door. "Come in."

Meghan peeked around the corner. "No microchip. Would you like me to have her bathed now?"

"Yes, please." He leaned forward resting his elbows on the desk. Telling Keira about the dog would probably be a bad idea. He needed to try to find the owner first and if he couldn't, he'd contact Keira. He wondered how she was doing.

Whoa.

Where had that thought come from? That little dog was messing with his mind.

"What are you going to do with little Blondie?" Meghan stroked the dog's back and she held her close.

Pete frowned. He'd really hoped it wouldn't come to this. "I guess I'll take her to the shelter."

Meghan pursed her lips. "You know…" She dragged the word out. "There's no reason we couldn't try and find her owner ourselves. We could put her picture on Craigslist, and hang up a flyer here and there around town."

"Meghan, if I took the time to do that for every stray that came into this clinic—"

"Hear me out. You clearly think a lot of this particular dog, and I don't blame you. She's very sweet. If you send her to the shelter she'll just be another lost dog. Take her home, Dr. Harding. Feed her and give her a warm place to sleep. I'll take care of finding her owners."

"But—"

"No buts."

He reached out for the animal. "Okay. I'll take her home. I'll need a crate and some sample dog food. I don't have anything at my house. I got rid of all my supplies back in Seattle after my German shepherd died." He removed Blondie from Meghan's arms.

"No worries. The clinic has everything you need. Just borrow the supplies for a few days." She nearly skipped from the room.

Pete stifled a laugh. He'd never seen his assistant so animated about anything. He knew Meghan meant well, but she wasn't considering his attachment to the animal.

The longer he cared for the little beagle, the fonder of her he would grow.

One good thing could come out of this. If Meghan failed to find the owner, he'd have an opportunity to see if the dog would make a good pet for Cody. Too bad he didn't know anything about the child other than his age. Maybe he should give Keira a call.

4

Keira sipped her morning coffee and leaned back into the comfy chaise while gazing out the window. Fresh snow covered the sidewalks and street, and wreaths and bells adorned the already beautiful buildings. Something about the German storefronts made her happy, and in spite of the snow they warmed her heart.

A smile touched her lips. Her favorite time of day was early morning when few people were out and about, but the Lighting Festival officially began tonight and the quiet would soon disappear. In anticipation of the crowds that would be flooding the small village, she'd asked Holly to work all weekend beginning at noon today. Thankfully the young woman had agreed.

Her thoughts shifted to her son. He'd asked her when he was going to get a dad again and she still felt at a loss as to how to answer. What she really wanted to know was what brought on the question.

Maybe tonight at dinner she'd find a way to ask Cody if he was missing his daddy. Of course he'd never really known him. He was only six months old when the accident happened. The only knowledge he had about Michael was from pictures and what she'd told him, which wasn't much. He'd only recently begun asking about his dad. Maybe he realized the other kids in his Sunday school class had dads and he didn't.

The phone blared into the silent apartment, causing her to jump and spill her coffee. "Oh, no!" She quickly set the mug on the counter and ran for her bedroom, ignoring her stinging hand. No way did she want Cody to wake up this early. She leaped across the bed for the phone before it rang again. "Hello." Her voice was brusque, but she didn't care.

"Keira, it's Pete."

"Oh." Her mind blanked. He was the last person she expected to hear from. She moved into the bathroom and ran her hand under cold water.

"Did I get you at a bad time? I wanted to catch you before you got too busy." He rambled on without taking a breath. "Josh said you're looking for a dog for Cody and asked for my help. I was hoping to find out a little about your son."

"Why?" Unease clouded her voice. Sure, they'd become friendly, but she had deliberately kept Cody away from the man. No sense in getting the child's hopes up—especially in light of his question about when he was going to get a dad.

"Maybe we should start over. I can't believe how badly I botched things between us when we first met, and you have every right to be wary. I'm sorry about that, Keira." Silence hung in the air between them like a great wall. "Do you want my help or not?" He asked softly.

Keira blinked, a little taken aback by his blunt question. "Well, I..." She really could use a professional's opinion on this. Taking on a pet was a big responsibility, one she didn't have time for. But she would make a sacrifice to please Cody. "Yes, Pete. I'd like your help, and starting over sounds good to me, too. What would you like to know?" After moving back into her bedroom, she spent the next five minutes answering questions ranging from Cody's activity level to his temperament. Meanwhile the coffee stain on the chaise was probably setting.

"Okay, I think I have all the information I need. Just one more thing."

"Shoot." She sounded more confident than she felt. Hearing his voice again made her pulse race and her brain a little mushy.

"Are you sure you want a dog? You work long days, and a dog needs attention—something he won't get while you're in the candy store."

She let out the breath she'd been holding. "That's a fair question. You're right, but this is important to Cody, and I'm willing to do what's necessary to make it happen."

"That's all I needed to know. It sounds like your son is ready for a pet, but I'd like to meet him to be certain."

"What?" Her voice rose a notch. "Aren't you being just a little ridiculous about this whole thing?" She padded out to the living room to deal with the coffee spill. "I mean, really, we are talking about a *dog.*" She kept her voice soft, so Cody wouldn't wake up. "It's not like I'm applying to adopt a child." Silence greeted her outburst.

Pete cleared his throat. "I didn't mean to offend you, Keira. I just want to make sure Blondie has the best home possible."

"Blondie? You already have a dog in mind?"

Pete cringed. He hadn't meant to say that. Maybe calling her was a mistake. He didn't know what had possessed him to contact her before he knew if the animal needed an adoptive home. It probably had to do with the fact that he really wanted an excuse to spend time with Keira. To see if what he'd been feeling was real. Although it didn't matter, since he shouldn't go there again with a single mom. What was he doing? He was setting himself up for heartbreak again.

He cleared his throat. "Maybe. I found a dog on the side of the highway last night. My assistant is trying to locate the owner, but for now I'm keeping the animal with me. She's a beagle. I'm guessing she's around three years old, and she is housebroken and very well mannered. I'm hoping we'll find the owner."

"Then why call me?"

"Because that way I'll know what kind of dog would work best for you and your son."

"Oh."

Did she sound disappointed? Had she hoped he'd

called for another reason? "Okay, I'll keep you posted, but please consider allowing me to meet your son. It really would help in finding the best fit for him."

"If you're going to the festival tonight, Cody and I will be there for the lighting ceremony. I decided to close at four so he can see Father Christmas ride in." The line went dead.

Pete looked at the phone a little surprised, then set the receiver down. In retrospect his questions had been somewhat obnoxious. Keira had every right to be annoyed with him. Even though he may have been premature in calling, he was doing it for the good of all involved. Too many people adopted animals with good intentions only to find out later they were a bad match.

He frowned. From what he understood, there'd be hundreds, if not thousands of people in the village for the festivities. No way would he be able to find the pair. Maybe he should plan to be at the store before closing to guarantee he'd be able to spend time with her. He glanced over

at the beagle sound asleep at his feet. Blondie really was a sweet dog. Whoever had lost her was probably full of worry. He'd call the shelter and let them know about her, just in case the owner checked there.

In the meantime he had work to do to be ready for tonight. He intended to make a good impression. There was no reason he couldn't be friends with Keira and her son. He ignored the sirens going off in the back of his mind, warning him that he was playing a dangerous game. Now to call the shelter.

"Hello, this is Pete Harding from the clinic in Leavenworth. I found a beagle last night along the highway and wanted to see if anyone has come by looking for her."

"Hi, Doc. Let me check." Dogs barked in the background and he could hear muffled voices. "Nope. Let me get your number, though, just in case."

Pete gave the number of the clinic and hung up. The idea that this dog could be someone's pet bothered him. He'd hate to turn the animal over to Cody only to have the owner finally show up and want her back. No kid should have to go through that. There were plenty of dogs that needed a good home.

"Go ahead and take off, Holly." Keira grabbed a disinfecting wipe and cleaned the counter. "As soon as I tidy up, we're leaving, too."

"Are you sure? I could keep the store open until the normal closing time."

"Thanks for the offer. But I don't want to leave you here alone." She also didn't like the idea of lost revenue, but it would be bad business to have an understaffed store. No, it'd be better to just hang a note on the door and close early. "We'll be working long hours until Christmas. Go and enjoy the festivities."

"Okay, thanks!" Holly draped her apron on the peg beside the storage room. "See you tomorrow."

"Bye."

Holly stopped outside and spoke briefly with someone before walking away.

Keira looked closer. "No. It can't be." *What is Pete doing here?* Did he really plan to attend the Lighting Festival with them? She never imagined he'd take her up on her comment.

After tossing the wipe in the garbage, she wrote the note for the door and frowned at her wobbly handwriting. She had to get it together. With paper and tape in hand, she walked to the door, flipped the sign to Closed and taped the note to the window. Her hands shook, and she clamped her jaw. A man should not have this effect on her, especially one who wasn't interested in her. She stepped outside. "Pete," her voice croaked.

He turned to face her. "Hi. I didn't know how I'd find you later, so I thought I'd wait for you here." His cheeks tinged pink and for the first time since she'd met him he looked uncertain. "I hope that's all right."

Keira nodded and opened the door. "Come inside while I lock up." Her heart raced and she willed her hand to stop shaking as she locked the door. Ignoring Pete the best she could, she called out to Cody, "Time to go upstairs." Cody appeared in the doorway holding a toy car in each hand. "Is it time for the festival. Momma?"

"Just about." She looked over her shoulder at Pete. "This is Dr. Harding. He's going to come with us tonight."

"And Aunt Susan?" Cody trotted to the stairs.

"Yes." She moved toward the stairway and looked over her shoulder at Pete. "You coming?" She turned and headed up without a backward glance, but heard his steps following close behind.

"If it's okay with you, your son can call me Pete. I don't know why, but I've never liked being called Doctor. I guess I always think of a medical doctor when someone says that, and since I'm not..."

Keira stepped over the threshold and waited for Pete to enter. "Sure. I need to change. If Susan comes, will you let her in?" At least she'd had time to pick up the clutter before work today. There was *one* thing to be thankful for.

"Okay." Pete stood with his hands in his pockets in the middle of the room, looking out of place in her small apartment.

Keira frowned. Too bad there wasn't more than one main living area. But this was it, a single room attached to the kitchen where the breakfast dishes still sat in the sink, waiting to be loaded into the dishwasher. Why hadn't she done them this morning?

"Have a seat. I'll be quick. Cody, maybe you can keep Pete company." She hustled to her room and slipped out of the German costume, then pulled on a pair of jeans and a red sweater. After running her fingers through her hair, she applied lip gloss. "What am I doing?" she whispered. There was no reason to primp for Pete.

Keira flung the door open and stopped. Cody and

Pete were on the floor playing cars. "No sign of Susan?"

"Nope." Pete glanced up, then made a car sound and raced his Mustang past Cody's Jeep.

Keira frowned. Pete's concern about getting hurt and missing his girlfriend's son came to the forefront of her mind. She didn't want Cody to become attached to Pete and get hurt the same way. Of course that was ridiculous. They'd never be around Pete enough for that to happen.

A knock at the door drew Keira's attention and she opened it.

"You ready?" Susan looked past Keira and her brows rose. "What's *he* doing here?" she whispered.

"He's coming with us." Keira ignored the shocked look on Susan's face and looked over her shoulder. "Grab your jacket and mittens, Cody. Aunt Susan's here."

The boy jumped up and clapped his hands. "Yay!" He snagged his coat from the back of a chair and slipped into his boots. "Let's go, Mr. Pete."

Mr. Pete? Made sense, since he'd been taught to address his Sunday school teacher in the same manner. Keira grinned. Her son was too cute. She squatted down and zipped up his jacket. "You ready?"

"Let's go!" Cody jumped up and down.

"Okay. Okay." She slipped her hand around his and motioned for her guests to go out first. "Be careful on the stairs, Pete. They can be slick."

"Thanks for the warning." He gripped the railing with his gloved hand, but took the stairs with ease.

Susan still wore the boot chains that she kept on her

56

shoes whenever snow covered the ground. "So, Pete, not to be rude or anything, but what are you doing here?"

"Susan!" Keira would've slugged her if she weren't going down the stairs and out of reach.

"Hey, I'm just curious."

Once they all stood safely on ground level, Keira noticed Pete's puckered brow. She didn't blame his hesitancy. It wouldn't be good to get Cody's hopes up about a dog. She shook her head slightly and looped her free arm through Susan's. "Cool it. I said I'd explain later," Keira whispered.

The foursome strolled out of the alley and up the street toward the gazebo and park where the festivities would take place.

"I can't believe all the people." Keira gripped Cody's hand tighter. No way did she want to lose him in this mob of tourists.

They crossed the street and got as close as possible, but found themselves stuck in the masses.

"I can't see, Momma."

Keira picked him up. "How's this?"

"No. Higher."

"I can't get you any higher."

"You want to ride on my shoulders, big guy?" Pete reached toward her son.

Keira held Cody closer. "He's fine."

"Higher." Cody stretched toward Pete.

The little traitor! Keira's stomach lurched. There was no sense in creating a scene. She allowed Pete to take Cody and watched as he carefully maneuvered her child onto his shoulders. Then it struck her. Maybe Pete had changed his mind about her. Maybe this was his way of showing her he was willing to take a risk on a single mom. Then again, maybe he really was just trying to help them find a dog. Cody clapped. "I can see! Thank you, Mr. Pete."

Pete chuckled. "No problem."

Keira sidled up to him and, standing on tiptoe, spoke into his ear. "Cool it. I don't want Cody to get attached to you."

He whipped his head toward her and whispered, "You're right. If you want I can leave now."

She saw horror in his eyes. Of course he'd be sensitive to this issue. After all, he'd experienced it firsthand himself. She hesitated. "Don't leave. I'm overreacting. Sorry." She sighed. "Cody has a prime seat."

"I understand. You're being a protective mom." He ducked his head and mumbled, "And I'm a protective pet lover. I'd do almost anything to make sure a dog is in the right home where he'll be safe and loved."

So that was his angle. The truth stung a little. She'd hoped he'd changed his mind about seeing her, but at least now she knew why he was here and it wasn't for her.

"Don't get me wrong, I wouldn't be doing this if I didn't like you, Keira. As a friend, of course." He kept his voice low. "I hope you don't mind, but I made reservations for a sleigh ride later this evening. I thought it'd be nice to get out of town, away from the crowd."

Keira's pulse raced. She couldn't leave the village. All

the sleigh-riding companies were outside the village. They'd have to drive, and fresh snow covered the streets. She sighed. Regardless of his motivation, she wanted to accept. It'd always been a dream of hers to ride in a horse-drawn sleigh. She opened her mouth but no sound came out.

"What's wrong?" Pete's brows pinched together.

"I'm sorry. We can't." Just then the countdown for the lights began, and then the village was aglow. The crowd erupted in applause.

Cody squealed his delight. "Look, Momma! It's Father Christmas!"

Keira looked up at her son's shining face and then at the man holding him. The child she understood, but the man baffled her. How would she make Pete see why they couldn't go on a sleigh ride without looking like a fool? Her stomach churned once again. This night was not turning out like she'd pictured.

5

Pete swung Cody off his shoulders. "Who wants roasted chestnuts and hot chocolate?"

"Me!" Cody raised his hand high.

Pete chuckled and looked to the women. He wasn't sure what had happened, but Keira, who already seemed leery of him, looked ready to bolt. "Susan, you're welcome to join us for the sleigh ride."

Susan glanced at Keira with raised brows. "That sounds like fun, but—"

"I said we can't go," Keira snapped.

Pete would've stopped and questioned her right then and there, but the crowd moved them along. The next thing he knew, Susan took his arm and spoke into his ear. "I don't know you very well, but my brother says you're a good guy so I'm going to help you out. Don't push Keira to go anywhere. She never gets in a car during winter. *Never.*"

"You've got to be kidding me." Why would someone go to such extremes? Something was definitely off with that woman. Thankfully Keira was taking Cody's picture with a nutcracker character and wasn't privy to their conversation.

"Since her husband was killed, she's changed. If you don't want to upset her more, forget about the sleigh ride...." Susan casually stepped away from him and swept up Cody in her arms as he leaped toward her.

How did she survive being so isolated? Pete grasped Keira's hand and pulled her toward the man selling chestnuts. "This way."

She tugged her hand away, but followed his lead and dragged her entourage along with them. "I've never had roasted chestnuts."

His eyes widened. "You've lived in Leavenworth for how long?"

"I usually close up my shop after work and hunker down for the night during December. I'm not much for crowds."

His heart melted a little with her admission. He understood what it was like to have a fear so overwhelming it affected your daily life. It seemed her husband's death had profoundly affected her ability to live a normal life. "I understand." He meant those words, too. His past had shaped him into the person he was, and he couldn't fault Keira for having her own issues. He'd really hoped to escape the throng of people on a quiet ride through the woods, but clearly that was out.

They stopped, and he purchased a few bags of chestnuts while Susan went for the hot chocolates. They found an out-of-the-way bench to sit on. "Are you sure about the sleigh ride? It's not that far from here. If I carried Cody, we could walk." It would be quite a trek, but he was willing to do it for Keira. She deserved to do something fun.

She hesitated for a moment, but ultimately shook her head. "I'm sorry. We can't."

At least Cody was intently enjoying his treat and not paying any attention to the adults. He'd hate to disappoint the child.

"Any word on the *d-o-g?*" Keira asked.

"Nothing yet. I'll let you know." So far Cody had impressed him with his good manners and overall enthusiasm for everything Christmas. The boy was a typical four-year-old overflowing with energy, but he also had a gentle spirit. Pete felt confident that Cody could handle a dog just fine, but sweet Blondie might be too timid for an active young child.

Keira shifted beside him. "This has been kind of fun." She plopped a nut into her mouth and grinned. "I can't believe I've missed out all these years."

Carolers garbed in Victorian clothing performed in the gazebo and music piped through speakers nearby.

"Only kind of fun?"

"Hey, I'm taking baby steps." She nudged his shoulder and smiled.

"Oh, in that case. Yes, it is nice." He cleared his throat. "Do you have dinner plans?"

She held up the hot chocolate and bag of chestnuts.

"I'll make mac and cheese for Cody later if he's still hungry, or maybe just a bowl of cereal. I've never been much of a cook."

"Cooking is a hobby of mine. You should let me whip you up something. It'd be my treat."

"Oh, no. I couldn't ask you to do that."

"You didn't. I offered." He nudged her shoulder like she'd done to him a moment ago. "Tell you what. You let me cook for you tonight, and I'll let you send me home with some of your famous chocolates."

Keira chuckled. "I'd be a fool to turn down a home-cooked meal I don't have to prepare."

He grinned and stood. "I'll run to the grocery store and pick up what I need, then meet you back at your place in, say, forty minutes."

"Sure. Come up the back stairs."

He nodded and strode for the clinic, where he'd left his SUV. What was he doing? He specifically avoided women with children and now he'd invited himself to Keira's place for dinner. Maybe he should call and tell her something had come up. Then again, it wasn't a date. Cody and Susan would be there. They were just a bunch of friends having a meal together, nothing more. Everybody needed friends.

Forty-five minutes later, Keira chewed her bottom lip and watched out the window for Pete. Where was he?

"Will you relax?" Susan stood and closed the blinds

facing the village. "He's probably trying to find a parking spot."

Keira sighed. "I'm sure you're right." She hated that she always thought the worst whenever anyone was late—a habit born from experience.

Footsteps on the stairs drew her attention. "Finally!"

Susan touched her arm. "Calm down or you'll scare him away."

Keira shrugged off the touch and scowled at her friend. "I'm fine."

"No, you're not. You're about ready to jump out of your skin."

Keira frowned. Maybe Susan was right. She'd never entertained a man at her home, and her stomach felt like she'd just gotten off a roller coaster. Oh, she knew he wasn't interested, but still she couldn't help the nerves. She shot up a quick prayer and took a few deep breaths, letting them out slowly.

A firm knock sounded on the door.

Cody jumped up. "I'll get it." He ran to the door and flung it open.

Pete stood there, his arms laden with three grocery bags.

"Oh, my. What did you buy?" Keira took the center bag. "Come in." She closed and locked the door behind him, then met him in the kitchen, suddenly embarrassed by the humble space. She looked at the galley kitchen and cringed, imagining it through the eyes of someone who enjoyed cooking. The stove top had only two working burners and the oven was smaller than standard. The fridge was apartment-size and the counter space was limited. At least there was a small eating bar and a window above the sink so she could enjoy the view outside. "It's not much, but it's served us well."

"It'll do." Pete pulled penne pasta and chicken from a bag, among other things. "Since you're not a cook, I wasn't sure what you'd have on hand." He chuckled softly. "I bought everything but the salt and pepper. I figured everyone has that."

Keira's face heated. "Umm. I hate pepper, so I never buy it."

He smacked his forehead dramatically. "Just teasing. No big deal. We'll do without."

"Are you sure? I know how you cooks can be." A teasing grin touched her lips.

"Would you like to help?"

Keira noticed Susan and Cody building a castle with blocks. "Sure."

"Great. I need a pot of water for the pasta and a pan to brown the chicken."

She opened the cupboard next to the stove and pulled out a stockpot and skillet. "Will these work?"

He grinned. "Perfect." He'd already started chopping the garlic and shallots.

"What're we making?"

"Chicken Piccata Pasta. I saw it on *Rachael Ray.*"

She chuckled.

"What?" He glanced her way, still chopping. "I've

gotten some of my best recipes from her show."

Laughing, Keira held up her hands in surrender. "You're not what I expected, Pete."

He shrugged and took the pan while she filled the pot with water. "There's a baguette in the other sack, along with the fixings for a green salad. Would you slice the bread while I brown the chicken?"

"Sure thing, but you're using my only cutting board." He scraped the shallots and garlic to the side. "Another crisis averted." He waggled his brows.

Keira laughed. "Again, you are *not* what I expected." Working shoulder to shoulder with Pete felt comfortable, but at the same time her heart raced. She reminded herself that he only wanted to see if they'd make good pet owners. There was nothing romantic about cooking with him. She sighed, unable to deny the truth—cooking with Pete was *very* romantic.

Cody dumped a box of blocks onto the floor, creating a crashing sound and startling Keira from her thoughts. She'd barely noticed Susan and Cody playing in the living room. Ah, reality. Pete wasn't interested in her, only in finding her son a dog.

"Everything okay?" He turned concerned eyes toward her.

"Fine."

"You sighed."

"Habit." It wasn't a lie. She sighed frequently, especially in winter. "Should I start the salad now?"

He dumped pasta into the boiling water. "Good

idea." She cleaned off the cutting board, washed the veggies and got down to business. "One chopped tomato coming up." She stabbed the fruit.

"Whoa! You're going to mutilate it, cutting like that. Let me show you." He took the knife and slid it through the tomato. "Now you try." He stood behind her as she placed the knife on the tomato. "Like this." He covered her hand with his. "Balance the tip on the cutting board and use a smooth rocking motion."

She held her breath, unable to breathe with his nearness. Following his instructions, she sliced through the red flesh.

"Good job." He removed his hand and stepped back to the stove. "The sauce is almost done and so is the pasta. Do you have a serving bowl?"

Afraid her voice would give away her nervousness, she pointed to the cupboard above the fridge where she stored the dishes she never used.

He pulled a yellow pasta bowl out and placed it on the counter beside the stove. "This looks brand-new."

She ducked her face and kept chopping. "I usually keep things simple. Serving dishes are extra work when it's just Cody and me."

A few minutes later they all sat around the table. Keira had to admit, her apartment had never smelled so good. She'd always loved the scent of cooked garlic.

"What is it?" Cody wrinkled his nose.

"Chicken and pasta." Keira took his little hand in hers. "Let's pray." She caught her breath when Pete's warm hand found hers for the second time that night. "Would you do the honors, Pete?"

He prayed and then they dug in.

In spite of Cody's disdain for the dish at first, he devoured his dinner. "May I be 'scused, please?"

Keira nodded. "Put your plate on the counter."

Susan cleared her throat. "This was delicious, Pete." She looked to Keira. "I hate to eat and run, but I need to head out."

Keira's stomach dropped. No way did she want to be alone with Pete. "Do you really have to go?"

"Sorry. I promised Josh I'd stop by tonight." Susan pushed back and reached for her plate.

"Don't worry about that." Keira stood and gave her friend a hug goodbye, whispering in her ear, "I can't believe you're leaving me alone with him."

"You're doing fine." She stepped back, said her goodbyes to Pete and Cody and then left.

Pete moved alongside Keira as she cleared the table. "Let me help." His hand brushed against hers.

A tingle zipped though her fingers up her arm. "I got it. You cooked."

He grabbed the serving dishes. "So did you."

At a loss for words, Keira allowed his help.

"I'll wash, you dry?" Pete filled the sink.

"Sure. Thanks for tonight, Pete. I honestly didn't expect you to show up this afternoon."

Maybe he'd been too hasty in declaring he never wanted to date a single mother again. No, he'd made the right decision, but he just wished he hadn't hurt Keira. He sensed she was still leery of him. At least she'd let her guard down a time or two tonight.

He finished washing the salad bowl and handed it to her. "That's it." He emptied the sink and sprayed the suds down the drain. "I'd planned to make dessert, too, but—"

"I couldn't eat another bite. Dinner was delicious and it didn't look too difficult, either. I think I might be able to make it on my own some time." She held up a finger. "I almost forgot. Stay right here." Keira disappeared through the doorway that led down to the store and reappeared a minute later with a box in her hand. "Chocolate, as promised." Pete grinned and took the candy. "I thought maybe you'd forgotten. Thanks."

"My pleasure, and thank you for the wonderful meal."

"You're welcome." He looked at his watch. "It's getting late, I should head home." After packing up the supplies he'd bought, he turned to Keira and kept his voice low so Cody wouldn't overhear. "I'm assuming you want the dog for Christmas."

"Yes, thanks. But if you don't think Blondie will work for us, we'll have to figure out a backup plan." She walked with him to the door.

"We'll see. Once I've had her a little while longer I'll be able to tell if they'd be a good fit or not. And her owner might still turn up." He looked down at her and searched her clear green eyes. They were filled with uncertainty. He wanted to reassure her that everything would work out.

She'd had enough bad stuff in her life. It was a good thing he held a bag because he was tempted to pull her into his arms. That would be a big mistake.

"Well, thanks again."

"Sure. I'll be in touch." He stepped down the stairs. One way or another he'd find a dog for Cody. That boy and his mom were growing on him in a big way and the sooner he found them a dog the sooner he could stop thinking about them. Maybe he should just give them Blondie. The dog was on the timid side, but Cody wasn't rough.

His cell rang. He pulled out his phone. "Hello."

"Dr. Harding, I'm calling from the shelter. A woman is here asking about a dog matching the description of the one you found."

His heart dropped.

6

"I'm telling you, Susan. Pete is a mystery to me. I can't figure the man out." Keira balanced the phone between her shoulder and ear while she finished stocking a shelf of prepackaged candy.

"What do you mean?"

"He says he won't date women with kids, but I feel a connection with him, and I don't think I'm alone. Then again, he did say he'd do about anything to make sure he matched a dog with the right people." She placed the last bag and strode to the door, flipped the sign to Open and unlocked the store. "I'm so confused."

"Has he called since Friday night?"

"No." Not that she expected to hear from him, but it would've been nice to know about the dog. She really did need to work on a plan B in case the beagle didn't work out.

"Hmm. I don't know what to tell you, Keira. Josh says Pete felt horrible about asking you out and then rejecting you because of Cody. Maybe he's just feeling guilty and is trying to be nice."

"Could be." She sighed. "I should probably just forget about him and his *d-o-g.*" Cody played in the storage room and might be listening. She lowered her voice. "I wish I could get over to the animal shelter and see what they have, but with my work schedule, it's impossible." Keira looked toward the window and shut her eyes to the snow. Maybe it would warm up soon.

"Why? You closed early to attend the festival. Why not do the same and go to the animal shelter?"

"I don't know." Christmas was still three weeks away. She had plenty of time. Then again, maybe Pete would come through after all. The bells on the door jingled as it breezed open, ushering in a woman talking on her cell phone. "I have to go."

"Okay, but Cody's going to have a wonderful Christmas with or without a dog."

"I know. Bye." She set the phone on the charger and smiled at the woman who bent to study the array of dark chocolates in the display case. Maybe Susan was right. She could close the store early on Tuesday since that was usually a slow day. But if she got his gift so soon, where would she keep it until Christmas?

Pete bumped into the dog crate on his living room floor and rubbed his shin. Blondie's owner had been ecstatic to have her back. Turned out Blondie's name was Lexie. He missed her. He eyed the crate again, remembering how the little dog had snuggled into his arms. It'd been a year since his German shepherd died. Maybe it was time to get another dog. Of course he still needed to find Cody a dog and phone Keira with an update. His stomach knotted at the thought of making the call. Would she be upset he couldn't give her son Blondie?

He had noticed a couple smaller breeds at the shelter in Wenatchee, but neither of them seemed right for the boy or his mother. Keira slipped into his thoughts way too often this weekend. A knock at his door startled him. He never had visitors.

Pete strode to the door and opened it. Two snowballs smacked him in the stomach. "Hey!"

Laughter filled the air.

"Come outside and play." Josh's older boy, Trent, hollered from his position behind his dad's Jeep.

Josh came around the corner of the house and reamed a couple snowballs Pete's way.

"Truce!" Pete shouted. "I'm not dressed for a snowball fight. How about you come in, and I'll make hot cocoa?"

Josh walked over to him and a grin spread across his face. "Sorry. The boys and I have always wanted to surprise someone like that and we hoped you wouldn't mind." He turned back to his kids. "I'll only be a few minutes. How about you play for a bit?"

The boys immediately ran for the biggest snowbank and started packing snowballs.

"We missed you at church today." Josh stood in the

entryway. "I tried calling you, but it went straight to voice mail."

Pete stopped brushing bits of snow off his shirt and looked at Josh. "Yeah. I had an emergency at the clinic and forgot my phone."

"I hope everything turned out okay."

Pete rubbed the back of his neck and looked away. "Not this time."

"I'm sorry. Sounds like a rough morning." Josh looked past him farther into the house. "Where's the little dog you told me about?"

"Her owner turned up."

"I suppose that's good." Josh rubbed his chin. "There's a family at church whose cocker spaniel had puppies a few months ago. They still have a couple and are anxious to sell them."

Pete raised a brow. "Really? Did you get their information? I'd like to contact them." Maybe he wouldn't have to give Keira bad news after all.

Josh grinned. "I figured you might. I left everything on your cell." He reached for the doorknob. "Looks like things are okay here, so I'll be on my way. Laura has a roast in the oven. You're welcome to join us."

"Thanks, but maybe another time." Pete followed Josh outside. He'd call and see about checking out the puppies later this afternoon. Maybe he'd get one for himself as well. A puppy would be more work, but there was something to be said for being able to train a dog from the start and not having to undo bad habits.

Two hours later Pete picked up a cute cocker spaniel puppy with light brown floppy ears and a white body with markings that matched her ear color. Her brother pawed up his leg. His coloring was slightly darker with similar markings. Pete put the dog down and the puppies rolled together in a tangle of paws and tails.

The owner stood off to the side. "Those two are practically inseparable."

"They do seem attached. I'm a vet. Do you mind if I do a quick exam?"

The owner shook his head. "Go ahead. They've had all their shots and the vet we use in Wenatchee said they're in excellent health."

Pete crouched down and scooped up the female again and performed a routine check of her eyes, ears and round belly, then repeated the process with her brother. Both dogs appeared healthy.

"Oh, I forgot to mention they're housebroken. Since it's so cold, we decided it'd be best to keep the critters in the house instead of the garage or outside."

"Good thinking." He stared at the pair and wondered if he should call Keira. Then he thought better of it. "What kind of deal will you give me if I take the pair?"

They agreed on a price. With a grin he pulled out his wallet. "I have a feeling one of these two will make a little boy very happy." He thanked the man, and he walked out to his car with both dogs tucked under his arms. If Keira decided she didn't want one of them he'd keep the pups for himself

After a trip to Wenatchee for supplies, he drove back to Leavenworth and parked behind Keira's store. He checked his watch—nearly six. She would be closing soon. He pulled out his cell phone and she answered on the second ring. "Hey, it's me, Pete. I'm parked behind your place and have a couple little friends I'd like you to see. Any chance you could come without Cody?"

Silence greeted him. "Um. Hold on a sec." She spoke to someone in the background. "Okay, Cody's covered. I'll be right there."

Two minutes later Keira trotted down the snow-cleared steps from her apartment.

He tucked the female into his jacket and stepped out of his SUV. "Over here, Keira."

Coatless, she hustled over, rubbing her hands up and down her arms.

"You must be freezing. I have a blanket in the car."

"Thanks, but I'm fine."

The puppy yipped and poked her head further out of his Jacket. "The beagle's owner claimed her, but Josh told me about someone selling these cocker spaniels. They're three months old, and the owner gave me a good deal. I bought the brother and sister and thought you might like one for your son." He named the price and handed the pup over.

"I didn't realize dogs were so expensive." The puppy licked her chin. Keira made a face, but giggled. "She's adorable." She handed her back. "You mentioned two dogs. Where's the other one?"

He opened the car door and allowed the male to leap out. He sank like a lead ball in the snow. Laughing, Pete picked the puppy up. "Careful, little fella." He held him out to Keira. "What do you think?"

"I prefer female dogs." Keira cradled the male to her chest and rubbed her cheek to his head. "But he's a sweet boy, isn't he?" She sighed. "I love them both and so will Cody. Whichever one you don't want. I'll buy from you." She bit her bottom lip. "It's supposed to be a Christmas present."

"No worries. I'll keep them both and deliver your choice on Christmas Eve."

Her eyes widened. "Really? That's so nice of you."

"No problem."

"Well." She looked toward her apartment. "Holly is closing the store and watching Cody for me. I should get back inside."

"Okay. I'll call you later." He watched her run up the stairs and wondered at the disappointment he felt. Now that he'd found Cody's dog, he wouldn't be seeing them much anymore, if at all—unless... An idea formed in his head and a smile lifted his lips.

Keira whispered into the phone and kept a close eye on Cody's door. He'd been in bed for an hour, but sometimes he didn't fall asleep right away. "Susan, you should see these puppies. They're adorable. I was a little surprised at the price, but after doing a search online I realized they were a bargain."

"Sounds like Mr. Toad has turned into a prince."

Keira cradled the phone tighter. "I don't know. He doesn't seem to want to be more than friends, but he's a nice man."

"Are you okay with that?" Susan never minced words.

"I wasn't to begin with, but yes, I think I am. Like I said, he's nice and I need all the friends I can get. My world has shrunk since Michael's death and, well. I'm ready to live again."

"It's about time!" Susan squealed. "I wish I were there right now. We'd celebrate. You've turned a corner, and I'm so proud of you."

"Thanks, but don't get all mushy on me." Keira folded her legs and tucked her feet onto the chaise. A slow smile lit her face.

"Remind me to thank Pete the next time I see him."

"For what?" Keira heard the surprise in her voice.

"For giving my friend back to me."

Had she really changed that much? Keira tucked that thought away for another time.

"Cody, please hurry. I don't want to keep Mr. Pete waiting." Keira tied a red scarf around her neck, then clamped her hands together to keep them from shaking.

Cody ran from his bedroom. "Okay, Momma. Let's go." She laughed. "Not so fast. We need to bundle you up. It's freezing outside."

Cody groaned and slipped on his mittens.

Her fingers tangled with his as she helped him zip his coat, then waited for him to tug on his boots.

"Ready!" He took her hand and pulled toward the door. "Are we late?"

"Not yet, but we'll need to hustle." Normally she'd have preferred the walking path down by the river, but the trek would be a bit far for Pete. She still couldn't believe he'd called and suggested letting Cody meet the puppies. They'd meet instead at the downtown city park on Front Street.

Keira locked up and trotted down the steps, holding Cody's hand. Thankfully the stairs only had a light dusting of snow and weren't slippery.

Cody jumped off the bottom step, pulling on her hand and dragging her forward.

"Slow down, buddy."

"Okay." He turned with hopeful eyes. "Will Father Christmas be in the park again?"

"Not this time. He only came for the Lighting Festival." Cody's shoulders slumped, and he kicked at the snow. "Oh."

"Don't worry. We'll still have fun."

"But there's nothing to do in the park."

"Not true." A smile touched her lips. Cody would be eating his words soon. They crossed Front Street and as they approached the gazebo, she spotted Pete. He had both puppies in his lap. Their blondish fur contrasted with the too-large doggie coats they each wore, one red, the other green. She held in a giggle. The man had no sense of style when it came to doggie clothes.

"Puppies!" Cody charged toward Pete.

Pete's eyes widened and he held the dogs tighter. "Whoa. Never run toward a dog."

Cody slid to a stop. "Sorry. Can I pet your puppies?" Pete's eyes crinkled when he smiled at her son. "Sure." Keira held her breath as Cody first patted the female's head, then the male's.

"What are their names?" Cody giggled when the dog licked his face.

"I just got them yesterday and haven't named them yet. I thought maybe you and your mom would help me decide." Cody tilted his head and pursed his lips. "Are they boys or girls?"

"One of each." Pete held out the female. "Would you like to hold her?"

Keira stepped closer to Cody and squatted beside him. "Be gentle."

"Look at her ears. Momma. She should be called Floppy."

"Hmm, that sounds more like a rabbit's name to me. What else can you think of?" She looked to Pete and noted the hint of a grin. "What do you think, Pete?"

"I have a few ideas. How about Molly, Sunflower—"

"Not Sunflower," Keira said. "It reminds me of the skunk in *Bambi*. Granted his name was Flower, but still." Pete chuckled. "Okay, Sunflower is out."

"I like Molly." Cody held up the female puppy and looked into her eyes. "Do you want to be Molly?"

The puppy barked and slathered him in kisses.

They all laughed.

"Sounds like a winner to me." Keira reached for the animal. "What about the boy?"

"I know!" Cody jumped up and down with his arm raised. "Charlie Brown."

"That's quite a name for such a little fellow." Pete picked up the male and studied his face. "What do you think, Keira?"

"It's up to you." She thought the name was cute, but it would be a mouthful.

Cody reached for the male. "How about Max?"

Pete shrugged. "I don't know. Max is a good name and would be easier to say, but a lot of dogs are called that." Keira watched her son and Pete interact. Their faces were so serious, like they were naming a new state or something.

Pete set the male dog on the ground.

Cody scrunched his face at the dog. "I think Max." He turned hopeful eyes toward him.

No way could he deny the boy. "Max it is."

"How about we let the dogs run around a bit."

Keira set Molly down beside Max and the two tumbled in the snow.

Cody giggled and his shoulders shook.

Pete drew a toy from his pocket and tossed it toward the dogs. Max clamped it in his jaws and chomped down, making the toy squeak.

"Can I try?" Cody reached for the toy in the dog's

mouth.

"Careful," Keira warned. "Some dogs don't like to share and may bite."

Cody yanked his hand back. "Please give me the toy. Max."

The dog tilted his head and blinked at the boy.

"Drop it," Pete said.

Max dropped the toy. Looked like the pup had more training than he'd realized. Good. That would make life easier.

Cody romped around in the snow with the puppies. Pete eyed the dogs. Which one would the boy connect with? The pups were such fun, and he'd hate to see either one go.

Keira sidled up to him. "Thanks for doing this, Pete. It was really nice of you."

"No problem." He explained what he'd observed so far about the animals.

"I was not looking forward to house-training a puppy, so that's a relief. I'd envisioned adopting an older dog." Keira's focus remained on her son.

"I can see why you'd like that option, but as long as you can take the puppy out every few hours during the day you shouldn't have any problems. I'll continue to work with both dogs until you're ready."

She nodded with a worried look.

Was she reconsidering? He'd better ease her mind. "I'll be sure to write out all the instructions you might need. Plus there are many websites with helpful information."

"I appreciate that."

Keira nodded when he spoke, but her attention kept drifting back to her son and the dogs, which gave him ample opportunity to watch her. The gleam in her eyes and the ready smile warmed him from head to toe even in the freezing temperature. Maybe he should ask her out after all and take another chance on love. "I was wondering—"

"Cody, I need to get back to the shop."

Shot down before the words even came out. Maybe it was a sign. The boy ran toward his mom and slid to a stop. His cheeks glowed from playing, and he beamed a smile at her. Pete longed to feel the same way. "Thanks for playing, Cody. Maybe we can do this again tomorrow?" He raised a brow at Keira and grinned when she nodded. "Same time?"

"Sure. See you then." Keira held out her hand to her son, and the pair marched across the street.

Pete attached a leash to each dog and walked back to the clinic with a little extra bounce in his step.

Later that same night Keira gazed out the window at the winter wonderland Leavenworth was known for. She could just make out the white lights decorating the top of the gazebo where Pete had met them several hours earlier. Maybe it was the puppies, but she sensed a change in Pete. She turned from the window, padded into her bedroom and noticed a piece of paper lying on the floor beside her bed.

Bending over, she snatched up the card and paused. The Christmas Surprise Ball was only two weeks away and she had yet to look for a dress. Maybe her mother-in-law had something she could wear. They were similar in height, but Mary was bigger-boned. A sigh escaped her lips as she opened her closet door and peered in.

Red fabric peeked out from behind rarely worn clothes in the back of the closet. "Oh, my! I forgot about that." She rushed to the never-worn dress and reached for the hanger. The deep red bridesmaid dress she'd purchased to wear in Susan's almost-wedding still looked perfect. She held it up in front of herself and light glimmered off the satin bodice and detailing. Beginning at the waistline, lace skimmed over satin and formed a delicate soft drape in front. She'd tried to return it years ago, but the place wouldn't take returns.

Would Susan mind seeing the dress again? The breakup had devastated her friend. Keira didn't want to dredge up bad memories.

Most women couldn't wait to toss out bridesmaid dresses, but this one was above average. Susan had planned a fairy-tale wedding theme, so unlike her normal style. But who wouldn't want to have a Cinderella dress? Unable to resist, Keira disrobed, stepped into the gown and zipped up the back. The mirror in her closet revealed it still fit like a glove. A smile teased her lips.

"Momma?"

Keira jumped and whirled around. "What are you doing out of bed?"

"I had to go potty, and I was thirsty." Cody rubbed his eyes. "You look pretty."

"Thank you. Did you get some water?"

He nodded.

"Good. Now go back to bed." She nudged him from the entrance of her closet toward the bedroom door.

"What's the dress for?"

"The Christmas Ball."

He stopped and looked up at her. "What's a ball?"

"Do you remember Cinderella when her fairy godmother gave her a beautiful dress and turned the pumpkin into a carriage?"

"Yes. She went to the castle. Are you going to a castle?"

Keira chuckled. "I wish, but no. This ball will be in the Festhalle."

Cody shrugged and padded to his room.

Keira slipped off the dress, carefully hung it back up and then pulled on her flannel pj's. After checking to make sure her son made it back to bed, she climbed into her own.

She'd originally planned to attend the ball for Cody's sake, but since kids weren't allowed it was pointless. Besides, she'd never be able to walk to the other end of the village without ruining the dress in the snow, not to mention the silver slippers that went with it. She rolled her eyes, imagining snow boots with the gown, although she could wear the boots there and change into the slippers later. As realization hit, a frown puckered her brow—she really wanted to attend, with or without her son. Something in her ached to be a princess for just one night. Too bad she didn't have a Prince Charming.

7

Pete glanced at the clock and hustled into exam room three. He'd have to make this quick if he was going to meet Keira and Cody in the park. A couple emergencies this morning had put him and Dr. Young behind schedule.

Thirty minutes later he draped the coats around Molly and Max and secured them under their bellies. After clipping on their leashes, he headed for the exit. If he hurried, he'd be only a little late. Stepping out the back door, the bright sunlight blinded him. When he'd come in to work it'd been dark. He slipped back inside to grab sunglasses from the edge of his desk.

"Oh, good. You're still here." Meghan took the dogs' leashes. "You're needed in room two."

"What's going on? I thought I was finished."

"So did I, but this person just walked in and requested to see you."

"Can't Dr. Young handle it? I'm meeting someone and I'm late."

"I think you should see this patient."

He frowned. "Fine, but after this I'm out of here." He dropped the sunglasses back on the desk, slipped on his lab coat, then strode up the hall. After a quick knock on the door, he walked in and plastered on his best smile. "Afternoon..." He stopped. "Blondie." He shook his head. "I mean—"

The woman chortled. "No worries. Doc. Lexie and I were in the neighborhood."

Blondie—er, Lexie, stood and quivered with excitement, then barked and jumped up.

He squatted before the dog and scuffed the fur on her neck. "It's good to see you, girl." He looked to the woman. "How's she been?"

"Missing you. I'd say. She whines all the time. This is the happiest I've seen her since she came home."

"She just misses my pampering. I'm glad you stopped by. Did you need anything or were you just saying hi?"

"That's it." The woman stood. "It appears her only problem was missing you. Thanks for seeing us."

"You bet." He pulled a liver treat from the jar on the table and gave it to Blondie. "She loves these." He stood with a sudden thought. "Be right back." He grabbed a small container of liver treats from the counter in front and returned to the room. "Give her one or two of these a day for a while and see if it improves her mood."

The woman took the small tub. "Thanks a million. Doc. I hope this works."

"Me, too." He walked them to the exit and waved to

the woman.

"Where's Mr. Pete?" Cody slumped on the bench and his lower lip protruded. "I want to play with Max and Molly."

Keira checked her watch again. "I know, honey." She looked toward the direction of the clinic. He could've at least sent a text if he wasn't going to show. Irritation soured her mood. She stood, holding her hand out to her son. "Come on. We're going."

"No! Mr. Pete said he'd be here." Cody crossed his arms and tucked his chin deeper into his coat.

"Excuse me?" she said in a warning tone.

Cody looked ready to cry. "Sorry."

"That's better. I know Mr. Pete said he'd be here, but he probably had something come up. We'll call him later and try to reschedule. Okay?"

Cody stood. "I guess." He took her hand and they tromped across the park toward Front Street.

"Would you like to go out for lunch?"

"McDonald's?" His voice lilted.

Keira frowned. She took him there at least once a week when the roads were clear, but it was too far to walk. "I'm sorry. I was thinking of getting soup."

"Oh."

"Don't leave!" a man hollered from a ways behind her. Keira turned toward the familiar voice and spotted Pete running toward them on the sidewalk slick with icy snow. He grinned and started to say something, but whatever it was got lost as his legs went out from under him, and he crashed to the sidewalk. The puppies bounced around and barked at him.

"Mr. Pete!" Cody yanked free, ran to the man, then pounced on his stomach and wrapped his arms around Pete as he lay prone. "You came."

Keira did her best to keep up and slid to a stop, nearly joining Pete on the snow-and-ice-covered walkway.

"Yeah, buddy. I made it. Sorry I'm late. Things at the clinic were a little busy."

"That's okay."

Keira lifted Cody off Pete and offered him a hand up. "You really shouldn't run on this stuff."

Pete stood. "Now she tells me."

"Are you hurt?"

"I'm fine."

"Can I play with Max and Molly?" Cody asked. "Sure, but let's play in the park. I don't want them to run out in front of a car." Pete took a hesitant step.

Cody nodded solemnly. "Okay. Can I hold a leash?" Pete looked to Keira for permission. Keira frowned. The puppies were little and probably wouldn't be able to break free of her son, but if anything happened to them... "I think Mr. Pete should hold the leash. You'll get plenty of time with the dogs in the park."

Cody scowled, but didn't argue. Keira walked beside Pete and kept an eye on Cody as he trotted his way back to the gazebo.

"Sorry I'm so late. I'm actually surprised you're still

here."

"A minute later and you'd have missed us. We were going to grab a bite before returning to the store. I'm afraid we only have about fifteen minutes. Holly has a class this afternoon."

"Guess we better make the most of this time, then." He reached down, removed the dogs' leashes and tossed the toy toward Cody. "Fetch."

The puppies tore after the squeak toy. Keira laughed. "They sure do like that thing. I hope I can find another one."

"Don't worry. I have an extra at home."

"Whew, thanks. You have a hard morning?"

"Busy. I was on my way to meet you when Blondie and her mom stopped in to say hi. Seems Blondie missed me."

"I can't imagine that." Keira gave him a teasing smile before turning and watching Cody. If she wasn't careful he'd think she was flirting. Who was she kidding? She was.

Fifteen minutes slipped by too fast. "I'll try and pick Cody's brain and see which dog he likes best. It's not fair to you not knowing."

"Don't worry if you can't get anything out of him. I think he's taken with both dogs still."

Keira raised a brow at his insight. For someone without kids he showed good skills at reading them. Then again, maybe it had something to do with the child he'd mentioned. "Cody, it's time to go."

Her son raced toward her with the puppies at his

heels. "Five more minutes?"

"Sorry."

Cody frowned and tucked his chin.

"I think Max and Molly enjoy your company." Pete attached the dogs' leashes. "We should plan to do this again soon. I'm tied up all day tomorrow, but maybe Thursday?" Keira nodded. "Same time?"

"Perfect." He walked with them to the sidewalk and waved goodbye.

"Mom?"

"Hmm?"

"Is Mr. Pete going to be my new dad?"

Keira caught her breath and felt her cheeks warm. She was quiet for a moment, hoping he'd move on to another topic. This was not a question he'd ever asked about anyone. When he looked up with puppy-dog eyes, she pursed her lips. "That's an interesting question. Do you want him to be your dad?"

He shrugged. "Yep. I like his dogs."

Her lips formed an O. As much as she wanted to know if that was all there was to his comment, she knew an opening when she heard it. "Which dog is your favorite?"

"Max."

"Really? Why?"

"He's a boy, like me."

A grin touched her lips. She'd give Pete a call tonight and let him know. "I see." They climbed the stairs to their apartment and went inside. She made them each a peanut-butter-and-jelly sandwich. "Will you pour the milk, Cody?"

He took the small pitcher from the fridge, grabbed two cups from the counter and took it all to the table. "Can I watch a video this afternoon?"

Videos were for special occasions, but he'd been so good today it was hard to resist his begging eyes. "Sure. We need to eat fast, then go downstairs so Holly can get to school."

"Thanks." He climbed into his chair, bowed his head in their silent grace and then dug in. Five minutes later, with DVD and portable player in hand, they trotted down the stairs.

Holly looked relieved to see them.

"Everything okay?"

"Yes. I was beginning to worry you wouldn't be back in time."

Keira slipped an apron over her white blouse and shook her head. "As long as I know your schedule, you have nothing to worry about. I won't let you down."

Holly grinned. "I appreciate that." She removed her apron. "How's Pete?"

"Fine. Cody enjoys playing with his new puppies."

Holly cast a knowing look over her shoulder. "Mmm-hmm. See you tomorrow." The bells jangled as she left.

For the second time that day Keira's mouth dropped open. What was with everyone today?

Later that night Keira cradled the phone to her ear.

"Hi, Keira. Everything okay?"

"Yes, great, actually. Cody told me that Max is his favorite."

"Good to know. Thanks. He's a great fit for Cody. Maybe I'll only bring Max to the park on Thursday. That way the two can bond without Molly interfering."

"If you think that's best. But doesn't Molly need to get away from the clinic, too?"

"It's good for the dogs to be apart. I'll have Meghan take Molly out."

"Who's Meghan?" Keira bit her lip. She sounded jealous. Was she?

He cleared his throat. "My assistant."

"Oh. That's good." She let out the breath she had been holding.

Awkward silence hummed over the line.

Pete cleared his throat. "Well, thanks for the call, and I'll see you Thursday."

"Okay. Bye."

Keira set the phone down and couldn't stop grinning. This would be the best Christmas Cody ever had.

Susan hung her coat on the hook by the door. "What's up? Why'd I need to come over today?"

Keira wrung her hands. "I wanted to ask you something in person." She'd gone back and forth in her mind about the ball several times and realized it was something she needed to do for herself

Susan squared her shoulders. "This sounds serious."

"It might be." Keira sat on the chaise and Susan perched on the edge of the couch. "You know how we all received invitations to the Christmas Ball?"

Susan nodded.

Keira licked her lips. "Well, with the roads covered in snow it's not likely I'll get out of Leavenworth until spring and ball gowns are not something anyone in town carries."

"True." Susan's eyes expressed confusion.

"I had an idea."

"Okay." She dragged the word out. "What did you have in mind and why are you so nervous? Just spit it out."

"I want to wear my bridesmaid dress from your wedding." The words came out like a runaway train.

Susan blew air out between her lips until the flow fizzled to a stop. "You mean my non-wedding. You still have that?" Vulnerability coated the words.

"Uh-huh. I didn't know what to do with it."

"You could have burned it." The hint of a teasing smile crossed her lips. "Well, don't keep me in suspense. Let me see it on you."

"Seriously?" Keira stood slowly. She thought for sure her friend would've at least thought about it for a minute or two. "Are you sure? I don't want this to stir up bad memories." Susan's fiancé's sudden change of heart just weeks before the wedding had done a number on her, and she'd tumbled into a deep depression for months.

"What's done is done." Susan's face brightened. "Now hurry up. I've never seen that dress on you. Remember it needed to be altered and you didn't want me to see it until it was perfect."

"That's right, I forgot." Keira hustled into her bedroom where the gown nearly covered her queen-size bed. In no time she had on the dress. She squeezed the full skirt through the doorway and twirled as she made her grand entrance. "Ta-da!"

Susan stood. "It's beautiful. You've got the curves, girl!"

"Just lucky, I guess, especially since I've had Cody."

"Wow. You have to wear it, Keira. It's amazing." Susan wiped a tear from the corner of her eye.

Keira went over and wrapped her arms around her friend. "I won't wear it if it makes you sad."

"It's okay." Susan blinked rapidly. "Seeing you in it reminds me of what could've been, but really, I want you to wear it."

"Maybe I should have the lace changed out or something to make it look a little different."

"What? Are you suggesting my taste is less than perfect?" Susan swiped at the tears leaking from her eyes and laughed. "If you don't wear this dress I'll never speak to you again."

Keira pretended to think about it, and Susan smacked her arm. "I'm serious."

"Okay. Okay. You win." Keira giggled.

"Good. Now go change before you ruin it."

"Bossy, aren't we?" Keira turned and tossed over her shoulder, "Be right back."

"Where's Cody?" Susan followed her to the bedroom door.

"Sound asleep. It'd take an air horn to wake him tonight." She quickly stepped out of the gown and slipped into sweats. "His grandparents took him skiing for the first time on Ski Hill, and he didn't stop talking about it until he fell asleep." The hill had been used as a ski jump, but now the locals swished down the slope. It was perfect for Cody and only five minutes away.

"You want coffee? I have a fresh pot."

"Sounds good."

Keira poured them each a cup, then snuggled back onto the chaise. Susan chose the stuffed armchair.

"How's the dog search going?" Susan blew on her coffee and glanced up with curiosity in her eyes.

Keira grinned. "Let's just say it's well in hand." She touched a finger to her lips, and looked toward Cody's room.

"I'm glad. How are things with Pete? I hear the two of you are spending time together."

"I imagine the rumor mill has been busy." Keira raised her brows. "Yes, we've met in the park a couple of times so Cody could play with Pete's adorable cocker spaniel puppies."

Susan raised her brows and quirked a smile. "Really?"

"That's it, so wipe those other thoughts from your head." She smiled, not really minding the teasing. "We're meeting again tomorrow. He's only bringing Max this time."

"Methinks there's more to the story than you're sharing." Susan wiggled her brows.

"Nope." If only that were true. She really liked Pete, and he seemed to like her, too, but no way would she throw herself at a man. She lifted a shoulder in a shrug. "Pete's a nice guy, but there's nothing more to it."

"Okay, whatever you say." Susan stood. "I should get home. I have to work in the morning."

"Wait. I know you said the ball isn't your kind of thing, but I was hoping you'd changed your mind. Any chance you're going?"

"Probably not. Why?"

"There's no way that dress would survive the walk. Did you notice how it drags on the floor?"

"I suppose you could drive."

"Yeah, right. We both know how that would turn out. I'd spend the evening paralyzed behind the wheel."

"True." Susan appeared to be thinking. "It's next week, right?"

Keira nodded.

"Let me think on it, maybe I can come up with an idea. But I'm still not sure about going. I'd need to find a dress and a date."

"You could come with me."

"You're seriously going to this thing alone?"

"I know. Totally out of character, but I really want to go"

"Okay. I'll get back to you. See you Sunday if not sooner."

8

Keira gave parting instructions to Holly, then grabbed the snow saucer and took Cody's hand.

"Will other kids be there?" Cody looked up at her with round eyes.

"Probably not. Christmas break starts next week." Keira kept her tone light.

He didn't seem to know if this news pleased him or not. She couldn't blame him. Fewer children on the hill meant he could sled more, but also meant there was a smaller chance he'd discover a new friend.

"But don't forget, Mr. Pete is bringing Max to play, too." She gave his hand a light squeeze. "Won't that be fun?"

Cody's face brightened. "What about Molly?"

"She's staying at the clinic today with Mr. Pete's assistant."

"That's nice of him to share." Cody's serious face looked up at her.

Keira chuckled. "Yes, it is." Her son was as precious

as they came. "Are you excited about sledding today?"

"Yep!"

In a few minutes they were at the park. It'd be a while before Pete showed, so they climbed the little hill.

"You want to go down together?" She held out the disk. "Yes." He bounced on his toes.

She sat and held out her arms for him to sit in front. "One, two, three!" She shoved off

"Wee!" Cody squealed as they raced down the short hill. Too soon the ride was over. "Wahoo! Let's go again."

"You want to do it by yourself this time?" She watched his face carefully.

He shook his head. "Go with me one more time." He held up a finger. "I'll go by myself next time."

"Okay." Keira raced her son to the top and seconds later they were gliding to a stop at the bottom. Cody stood and grabbed the disk and ran to the top again, then soared back down.

"Mr. Pete's here!" Cody abandoned the hillside and ran to greet Max. He flopped to his knees and let the dog kiss his face.

Keira cringed—gross. She'd have to talk with Cody about that later.

"Looks like you're having a lot of fun sledding." Pete handed Cody Max's toy. "Maybe you and Max could ride down together."

"Yeah! Come on. Max."

The puppy chased after her son.

"That's too cute. I wish I had my camera." Her

phone had one, but it was old and lousy.

Pete pulled his phone out and took a couple of shots. He tilted the screen toward her. "How's this?"

"Love it. Will you send me those?" She stuffed her hands in her jacket pocket.

"Sure." He snapped a close-up of her.

"I do *not* want to see that one." She laughed.

"Aww, it's not that bad. In fact, I think it looks good." He held out the phone for her to see.

"You need glasses." Keira followed him to a bench. After brushing snow off, they sat. "Was Molly upset when you left with Max?"

"She yipped some, but not too bad. Meghan gave her a treat and is taking her for a walk."

"You have a thoughtful assistant."

His silence unnerved her. Was there something between Pete and Meghan? What did it matter if there was? There certainly wasn't anything between the two of them, other than a little puppy. "Do you still think you can bring Max by on Christmas Eve?"

"I don't see why not. Do you have all the supplies you need?"

"Not yet." Keira frowned. That was one hurdle she hadn't figured out how to jump. The pet supply store was in Wenatchee, and as much as she wanted to, she couldn't bring herself to drive there. She'd even gone so far as to ask Holly to run the shop alone for a couple hours, but when it came to getting behind the wheel, she froze in fear. Passersby probably thought she was a lunatic just sitting there for twenty minutes talking to herself.

Susan's words came back to Pete and he wanted to kick himself for not remembering sooner—Keira was terrified of driving in the snow. "You know, I go to Wenatchee at least once a week. If you'd like to come along you could pick up what you need. Of course the clinic carries the basics like food, but none of the fun stuff."

Keira bit her bottom lip. "Thanks. Um...I'll let you know."

"Mind if I ask you a personal question?" He watched her face closely and saw a flicker of surprise.

Keira shivered. "Ask away, but I don't promise to answer."

Pete had a sudden urge to pull her close to help keep her warm, but thought again. He didn't want her to get the wrong idea. But was it the wrong idea? Over the past week he'd come to look forward to their time in the park and visiting with her. "I was wondering about your fear of driving in the snow."

She caught her breath. "That isn't something I care to discuss."

"I understand, but how do you function?"

"I make do. My in-laws help out a lot and Susan delivers groceries once a week."

"I see." Seemed to him the people in her life were enabling her fear. But who was he to judge when he had his own issues? "I could pick up the supplies." There, it was out. Would she resent his offer?

She turned startled eyes toward him. "You'd do that for me?"

"Of course. I don't want Max to go without."

Disappointment clouded her eyes. What had he said wrong? He pulled her into a quick side hug, unsure how to undo whatever he'd done. "I need to head back to the clinic. If you want my help, let me know."

"I'd appreciate it, thanks. But don't go overboard. Our apartment is small."

She was right about that. It was a good thing Max would never be too big, or he'd be miserable in the small space. He waved Cody over to them.

The child ran, but the puppy beat him. Max barked at Pete. "What's up, little guy?" He bent down and attached the leash. "I'd suggest meeting tomorrow, but the festival begins again."

"Yeah, but Cody will sure miss seeing those two. Maybe you could come to our place for dinner and bring Max and Molly along." Keira took Cody's hand.

"I thought you didn't cook."

"I'm not a gourmet but I make a mean lasagna. How about six-thirty tomorrow night? That'll give me enough time to get it in the oven and clean up a little after work."

"Sounds great. See you then." He turned and walked back to the clinic with an extra bounce in his step. Something was happening between him and Keira. He couldn't exactly name it, but something had changed.

Five minutes later he strode into the clinic.

Meghan breezed by him, holding Molly. "She's such a doll. I can see why you got her."

Pete followed with Max and put the dogs into a kennel. "Yeah. They're both pretty special."

"Oh, I almost forgot. I was looking for a file in your office and found this." She pulled a card from her oversized pocket.

He took it. "Thanks."

"Aren't you going to open it?" Her eyes lit.

He shrugged and slid his finger across the top. Inside he found a vellum card and a ticket. He pulled it out. "What's this?" He read the contents, then tossed them into the garbage.

Meghan snatched the ticket. "What are you doing? Don't you know that only two hundred of these went out?"

"You want the ticket? Go for it."

"I think you should attend. It's the social event of the year."

Pete tuned out his assistant. Of course Meghan would know all there was to know about the ball. She seemed to have her finger on the pulse of everyone and everything. Well, he was not going regardless of how many people were invited. He hadn't waltzed since middle school PE and had no intention of starting again.

Meghan brushed past him. "I'll hang this on your board. At least think about it."

He didn't bother to stop her. He slipped into his lab coat and wondered for a minute if Keira would be attending the ball. Not likely, since she didn't get out much. From what he'd gathered from Josh, this holiday season was the most Keira had been out since her husband's death.

It was kind of sad, really. A beautiful young woman holed up in a shop day after day, year after year, never enjoying life. A thought occurred. "Meghan!" He turned and bumped into her. "Sorry, I didn't know you were there." He shared his thought with his assistant, then rocked back on his heels, waiting for her reaction.

She looked shell-shocked. "I love it, but I can't believe *you* thought of it." She gave him a teasing grin. "I'll get right on this and let you know what I come up with."

"Thanks."

She winked at him and hustled into his office.

He felt his cheeks warm. He hoped he hadn't made a mistake trusting Meghan with such an important task. This was clearly outside her job description. He moved to tell her never mind, but when he saw the animated expression on her face, he couldn't. He ran a hand along his neck and pondered his sanity. What had come over him? Ever since he'd met Keira, his world had been turned upside down.

"Susan, I need your help." Keira spoke into the phone keeping her voice low, so Holly and her customer wouldn't hear. "I invited Pete over for lasagna tomorrow night, and I'm out of the noodles. Would you have time to stop and get some?"

"Sure, but not until tomorrow. I'm hosting my Sunday school class tonight. Do you need anything else? Salad, bread, dessert?"

What had she been thinking, inviting Pete to dinner? There was way more to planning a meal than she'd thought. Plus Cody would be starving and ready for bed by the time the lasagna finished cooking. "I'll get the dessert and bread from the bakery, but if you could take care of the salad and noodles, that'd be helpful."

"Will do. See you tomorrow."

"Okay, thanks." She hung up the phone and checked on Cody. As she'd predicted, he'd zonked out on the cot she'd finally been able to set back up in the storage room.

Keira slipped an apron over her head and moved beside Holly. "How's it going?"

"It's been a little slow, but we had steady customers the whole time you were out."

Keira grinned. "Well, it doesn't hurt that you're so cute." Her accounting showed that sales were great when Holly was manning the counter. "I think my customers like you. I hope you'll consider coming back next year."

Holly's eyes shone. "I'd like that, but it'll depend on my schedule."

"Looks like everything is under control out here. I'll be organizing stock if you need anything." Keira's mind drifted to her dinner plans with Pete. Too bad Susan couldn't drop the pasta by tonight. She'd be able to get everything ready ahead of time and just pop it in the oven.

Oh, well. Her stomach fluttered just thinking about Pete.

Pete parked behind Keira's building and scooped up the puppies, one in each arm. Molly licked his face and he lifted his chin to avoid a direct hit to the mouth. The clock on the dash read 6:20 p.m.—a little early. Maybe he should walk the dogs a bit first. Then again, what were ten measly minutes?

He stepped out, pressed the auto-lock key and carefully climbed the stairs. It'd snowed earlier and a couple inches of fresh powder covered the steps. A light shone in the kitchen window where Keira stood holding a glass to her lips.

She waved and a moment later the door opened just as he reached the top. "You made it." She stepped back, allowing him to enter. "Go ahead and put them down. Cody is finishing up with his bath, and then I promised him a little playtime with the puppies."

"He isn't joining us?"

"I'm afraid not. He had a fun day snowmobiling with his grandparents, and he's pretty wiped out. Besides, I like him to be in bed by seven, so he ate earlier."

"You let him snowmobile? I'd think you'd be afraid to allow that."

"I know, but they are very careful and it's not like they're doing it where it's dangerous. My mother-in-law, Mary, said I shouldn't smother Cody, and she's right." Keira moved into the kitchen. "I was just putting together the salad. Lasagna will be ready in a half hour. Sorry it's so late, but I figured if you're starving, we could start with salad and French bread."

"Sounds good to me." Pete followed the pups around the apartment, making sure they stayed out of mischief. A few toy cars and a pile of blocks were scattered near the window. He reached down to pick up the toys.

"You don't have to do that. Cody will clean up when he comes out." She set a basket of bread on the table.

"I'm afraid one of the dogs will chew on something and choke."

"Oh. I didn't think of that." She frowned and looked around the small space. "I suppose I'll need to get a few bins with lids."

"That'd be a smart move."

The bathroom door opened and Cody came out in bare feet and car-printed pajamas. "Hi, Mr. Pete." His face lit. "Max and Molly!" He dropped to the floor and scratched each dog on the back.

Pete raised a brow toward Keira.

"I wanted the dogs to be a surprise, just in case your plans changed." She walked over to her son and squatted beside him. "Puppies are like toddlers. They pick up things with their mouths and could choke. Will you please put your toys away before you play with the puppies?"

Cody scrunched his nose. "Jacob stuffed a bean up his nose in church. Will they put stuff up their noses, too?"

Pete chuckled. This kid was too much. "They'd need

fingers to do that. Want some help putting your blocks away?"

"Sure. I bet I can put more away than you." Cody scooped handfuls as fast as he could into a box.

Pete found the strays and tossed them in.

"I win!" Cody raised his arms above his head. "Now can I play?"

Keira nodded. "Just don't get them too excited. We don't want any accidents."

Pete meandered to the front window that overlooked Front Street. "This is a pretty nice setup. I wasn't paying much attention the last time I was here." The sides of the apartment were windowless, but the back overlooked the alley and had a river view in the distance. The bedrooms occupied one side of the space and he assumed each had a window, one facing the front, and the other the back with a bathroom in the middle.

She came up beside him and looked out the window. "Thanks. It's home."

Thirty minutes later she convinced Cody the puppies had to go to sleep, so it was time for him to go to bed, also.

"I'll be right back." Pete leashed the dogs and strode to the exterior door. He returned several minutes later holding a large round dog bed under an arm and the dogs' leashes with his other hand. "I thought this would be a good idea."

The puppies circled, then snuggled together on the large pillow.

"They're adorable." Keira grinned and cut into the

lasagna. "You ready for dinner?"

He'd been ready for hours. "Sure." He moved into the kitchen and sniffed the pan of hot pasta. "Smells good."

Keira slid a generous slice of steaming lasagna on a plate and handed it to Pete. He closed his eyes and inhaled. She chuckled to herself for a second, she wasn't sure the food would make it to the table before he took a bite.

"Thanks." He took the plate and sat.

Keira sat across from him, her stomach a bundle of nerves. Hopefully the food would taste as good as it smelled.

Pete offered a blessing, then forked a generous amount into his mouth. Keira watched his face for a clue to what he thought. He chewed slowly with the hint of a smile. *Yes!* His gaze slammed into hers. She looked down and took a quick bite.

Pete cleared his throat. "Have you heard about the Christmas Ball?"

Keira choked on her lasagna and nodded. Her eyes watered and she reached for her glass of water.

"You okay?"

"Fine. Sorry." Why would Pete bring up the ball?

He studied her a moment longer as if to assure himself she really was okay. "About the ball. I think it could be interesting, and I was hoping you'd accompany me."

Keira's eyes widened. This sounded like a date, and

he'd been very clear on that issue. "I thought—"

"I know. But this would just be two friends going together, having a fun time."

Keira frowned and picked at the lasagna, then took a long drink of water. If she told him she might be going with Susan, it'd sound like she wasn't interested, but at the same time she couldn't uninvite her friend. She finally set her glass down. "I already asked Susan to go with me, but to be honest it's doubtful she'll come."

"We could all go together. Unless of course you'd rather not." He raised a brow.

"I think it'd be fun to go together." Just so long as she could keep her heart intact. No way could she fall for him. Who was she kidding? He was her knight in shining armor—scratch that—slightly tarnished armor.

"Great." His eyes lit with satisfaction, and then he shoveled a forkful of pasta into his mouth.

"Yeah." She'd have to call Susan and fill her in, and she still needed to find a sitter. She didn't want to bother her in-laws again, but Cody would be most comfortable with his grandparents.

"I'm working on a surprise for you."

"Seriously?" A chill shot through her. She gave herself a mental shake. It was probably no big deal, but the look on his face said otherwise. Talk about sending mixed signals. They were just friends. He'd said so himself. She appreciated that he desired her friendship, but could her heart handle just friendship with a man she was so drawn to?

Pete pushed back from the table and patted his flat stomach. "That was delicious. After a meal like that, it's hard to believe you don't consider yourself a cook." He glanced at his watch. It was only eight, but maybe he should take off since Cody was sleeping. He'd noticed the child's door stood ajar, and he'd hate to wake him.

"Thanks." She grabbed the salad bowl and breadbasket and took them into the kitchen. She covered the leftover lasagna and put it in the fridge.

Pete grabbed their plates and rinsed them in the sink. "I have a recipe for chili that's impossible to mess up."

She wrinkled her nose. "Cody won't eat beans."

"That's too bad." He checked on the puppies and grinned. The duo snuggled together on the dog bed, sleeping like the dead. "Thanks for having me over tonight, but I should probably head out. I know you have early mornings."

Keira nodded. "I do, but there's no reason to rush off, unless you're in a hurry."

He shook his head. "I'm not."

"Good. I picked up apple dumplings from the bakery up the street. You're going to love them. Just let me pop them into the microwave. They're much better warm." Pete sat at the bar and watched Keira load their plates into the dishwasher and grab dessert dishes from the cupboard. He hadn't anticipated her already having plans for the ball. It seemed out of character for her, but what did he know. At least his surprise could accommodate a third person. It was a shame he wouldn't have Keira all to himself, though. Then again, it was probably for the best. He trusted Keira as a friend, but beyond that was still a struggle. Although the more time he spent with her the more he wanted to forget about his dating rule.

Keira handed him a bowl and spoon, and then curled up on the chaise. He settled into a nearby chair. The only sound in the room was the gentle snores coming from the puppies.

Keira cleared her throat. "I'm a little confused about something. You made it very clear that we have no future as a couple, but yet every time I turn around, there you are."

Pete raised a brow. "I also said I'd like to be friends."

"This feels like more. What's going on, Pete?"

Whoa. He dropped his eyes to the bowl and slowly dug into the dumpling. He stopped and pushed the bowl aside. "I don't know what you mean. I'm only trying to be your friend."

"Friends don't usually date."

"Okay, but they hang out. We're just two friends attending a community event together." He shrugged. "If you'd rather not go to the ball with me, that's fine." He held his breath, hoping she wouldn't back out.

She cut her dumpling into smaller and smaller pieces until it resembled chunky applesauce. "I didn't say that. I'm just confused."

"That makes two of us." He rubbed the back of his neck. What was he thinking? Had he become obsessed with helping her because he felt bad about her driving

113

phobia? Or was what he felt for her more than that? He shrugged. "I like you, Keira—a lot, actually. I want us to be friends." Keira stared at her dessert. "I'm sorry. I guess I overreacted."

"Are we still on for the ball, or would you rather not go with me?" He wasn't sure he cared to hear her answer right now. He stood and took his half-eaten dessert to the kitchen. Turning, his hand knocked the dish Keira carried, nearly dislodging it from her grasp.

Keira caught her breath and managed to stop before plowing into him. "Whoa!"

He reached out to steady her. "You okay?"

"Mm-hmm, and yes, I would like to go with you."

A grin slipped into place. "I'm glad. I'll get back to you with the details. Meet me and the dogs in the park on Monday?"

"Sure." Her gaze captured his and held. "That's becoming Cody's favorite thing to do. He really looks forward to playing with those rascals."

Pete realized his hand still gripped her arm. He touched his thumb to her cheek and tucked a strand of hair behind her ear. Her lips parted slightly and drew him to her like a magnet. Would her lips be as soft as her cheek? Leaning toward her, he tilted his head. "You have the most incredible eyes."

She sucked in a breath, and he stopped inches from her face.

"Keira?"

Confusion filled her eyes where light had sparkled

just seconds ago. She took a step back. "Funny, I remember thinking the same thing about your eyes." She breezed past him and set her dish on the counter. "Would you like help with the dogs?"

"Ah. No, but thanks." He clamped his jaw. What had he just done? Had he destroyed their fragile friendship before it even had a chance? Time to vacate before he did something even more stupid.

Keira wrapped a blanket around her shoulders and sat in the darkened room lit only by Christmas lights. Tears meandered down her face and dripped from her chin. Her nicely ordered world was spiraling out of control much like the snowflakes outside. It was all Pete's fault! That man mixed her up beyond words.

She'd thought for sure he was going to kiss her tonight, but that was crazy. He was very clear he only thought of her as a friend. He'd certainly said it enough times. Her heart ached from the loss of her husband, but something new had begun to fill its place. Or maybe it was *someone* new, and that terrified her. Especially since he wasn't interested.

She shuddered and hugged her knees to her chin. She couldn't allow Pete into her heart. If she let him in and he walked away he'd hurt her and Cody. They'd lost enough already.

9

Pete tapped a pen against the file. "Well?" He leaned forward and rested on his forearms.

"Everything's set. Oh, and I was able to clear your schedule so you can go to that conference in Seattle tomorrow." Meghan cuddled Molly in her arms as the puppy licked her chin. She tilted her head back and giggled. "That tickles."

"Great! Now I just need to find a dog sitter."

Meghan backed away. "Don't look at me."

"Maybe Keira can help me out."

"Good thinking. After all, this will give her an idea of what she's in for. Besides, once you tell her about what you have planned there's no way she'll say no."

"Except it's a surprise." Pete grinned, then sobered. What he was trying to do for Keira felt like mountain climbing in a blizzard but it was worth it. He pushed back from his desk and stood. What if she hated his surprise? "Maybe my surprise is a bad idea."

"No, it isn't." Meghan set Molly down. "I don't want

to speak out of turn, but you are one boring man. This is the most life I've ever seen in you. Whoever this woman is, she's good for you. You're not canceling."

"Ouch." He grinned. He wasn't boring. She just didn't know him outside of work. He hiked and skied among a plethora of other outdoor activities, although he usually did those things alone.

Meghan bit her lip and shook her head. "Sorry. My mom says I'm too blunt for my own good."

"No problem. Will you keep Molly during lunch today?" He took Max out of the kennel, attached the green coat around him and then latched his leash.

"Sure. She's such a sweet thing, and it's good for these two to spend time apart. Come Christmas they're going to miss each other."

"Yeah." He'd thought of that several times, but in the back of his mind he hoped to continue meeting Keira in the park, and the dogs would see each other then. But maybe that was unrealistic.

With a sigh, he plunged into the cold winter day. Snow swirled around his boots as he walked toward the village park. The clip-clop of horse hooves on the cleared road drew his attention. A large black mare pulled tourists through the village in an open-top carriage decorated for Christmas with a small round wreath and red flowers. He grinned and waved to the driver.

Christmas music piped through nearby speakers and rosy-cheeked shoppers strolled along the sidewalks. Ah, Christmas in Leavenworth couldn't be beat.

"Mr. Pete!" Cody ran toward him.

Max barked and pulled at his leash.

"Slow down, Cody. Remember never to run toward a dog."

The child slowed to a walk. "Sorry. I forgot."

Pete looked for Keira but didn't see her. "Where's your mom?"

Cody pointed toward the gazebo. "May I hold Max's leash?"

"Sure." Walking beside the boy, he imagined this was what it would've felt like if Jack had still been in his life. His shoulders slumped. He missed the child. It'd been a year since he'd seen him, but he still loved him and imagined Jack would always hold a place in his heart. But maybe it was time to let go of the past.

Cody slipped a small hand into his. "Yesterday I helped decorate Grandma and Grandpa's tree. It was so cool."

"Really? Did your mom help?"

Cody frowned. "No. She worked at the store." He tugged on Pete's hand and motioned for him to come down to his level. "I think Mom's afraid of snow."

Pete squatted beside the child. "Why do you say that? I saw her playing in it with you just last week."

He shook his head. "I meant driving in it. She never goes anywhere unless we walk, not even on Thanksgiving. She gets a scared look on her face whenever she looks at our car. Grandma says it's because my dad was killed driving on a snowy road."

"I see. I'm sorry about your dad."

Cody shrugged. "I don't remember him."

He patted the boy's shoulder and stood. Keira waited on the edge of the snow-covered grass with her hands tucked into her jacket pockets. She got closer with each step. Pete slowed. He needed to know just how severe this phobia was and if it applied to *all* modes of transportation, because if it did, his plans for the ball were ruined.

He released the leash from Max's collar and let the child and dog play.

"Hey there." Keira smiled up at him.

He sat beside her on the bench. "Hi." He wasn't sure how she'd take his meddling, especially after Friday night. In fact he was a little surprised she'd shown up here at all.

"No Molly today?"

"I thought it best to leave her at the clinic. Max needs time alone with Cody."

Keira nodded and sat silently beside him.

He crossed his arms, suspecting he knew the reason for Keira's unusual quiet. "About Friday night." He sensed her shift his direction and felt his face warm. He didn't want to have this conversation. It wasn't as if he'd kissed her. They'd shared a moment—that was it.

"Yes?"

He rubbed the back of his neck and glanced at her. "I'm not good at this."

She gave him an encouraging smile. "Try."

He focused on Cody and Max as they slid down the hill on the child's snow saucer. "I'm sorry about crossing the line." There, he'd said it.

"You mean when you almost kissed me?"

Did she really say it? "Ah. Yes."

"I'm confused by whatever is going on between us."

"What do you mean?"

"I'd like to understand your intentions. I hear what you say, but you're sending mixed signals." Her voice was tight.

Oh, boy, he'd done it now. He took a deep breath of cold air and let it out slowly while gathering his thoughts. They say honesty is the best policy and he was too old to play games. Keira seemed like a woman he could be straight with. "It's like this—the first time I met you I was attracted to you." He glanced at her and saw the surprise and pleasure in her eyes. "I actually wished I could get out of my blind date and take you instead." He smirked. "Of course, I didn't know you were my date. Then, when we had coffee, I was even more attracted to you." He paused.

"Go on," she encouraged softly.

"When you mentioned your son, I panicked." He shrugged. "I'd planned to stay out of your life, but then Josh said his sister asked for help finding a puppy for Cody. I have a soft spot for animals and couldn't resist helping. I really like you, Keira. I enjoy being with you."

"What does that mean for us?"

He took a deep breath and let it out slowly. "For now. I'm still not willing to commit to anything more than friendship. I got caught up in the moment and was out of line. I'm very sorry." He spoke the words softly. The pain etched on her face nearly did him in, but she quickly shuttered her feelings.

She looked toward Cody. "Okay, friends it is. But no more almost-kisses."

He ached to draw her close, but common sense ruled. "Got it." Pete shifted, leaning forward, and rested his elbows on his knees. "Cody is doing well with Max."

"Yes, he is, isn't he?" Pride filled her voice. "I can't thank you enough for your help, and for the record, I appreciate your honesty regarding—" she hesitated "—us."

"Sure." But was he being completely honest? His brain said he only wanted friendship, but his heart wanted more. Ugh, what a mess.

"Um. Do you still want to take me to the ball? Susan decided not to go."

He raised a brow. "Of course."

"Oh, good. I'm so intrigued by the idea of an old-fashioned ball that I can't stay away, but I really don't want to go alone."

Pete leaned back and relaxed. It seemed things were normal again, and normal he could deal with. No more awkward conversations! "I saw the weather forecast and other than tomorrow it's not supposed to snow."

She started. "That's great news. I noticed the roads are clear, too. Maybe I'll even be able to get to the grocery store."

He raised his brows. This driving-in-snow phobia was a serious problem.

"In case you haven't noticed, I'm a bit of a mess when it comes to winter driving."

"I've noticed. If there's anything I can do to help, please let me know."

"Thanks, I think this is something I need to deal with on my own." She waved Cody over. "Time to go, kiddo."

"Wait. Before you leave I was wondering if you'd be able to pet sit for me. Every now and then I like to attend a conference and there is one in Seattle tomorrow. Sorry about the short notice, but I wasn't sure it would work for me to attend until today."

Cody jumped up and down. "Please say yes!"

She looked from one hopeful face to the other. "Okay."

"Yay!" Cody wrapped his arms around her legs. "Thanks. I thought I'd head out this evening if you're okay with that. I'd like to try to beat the weather that's heading our way."

She shrugged. "Okay. Are you sure about going? The roads will be a mess."

"That's why I'm leaving early. I'll bring the dogs by when I'm off work. I can't thank you enough."

"Don't mention it." She shot him a nervous smile.

He ignored Keira's obvious discomfort with the situation. It would be good for her to have the puppies—a trial run of sorts. Better for her to find out sooner than later if owning a dog would work.

Keira rushed through the store toward the stairs that led to her apartment. It was time to let the pups out. "I'll be back in five minutes."

"No problem." Holly waved her off.

Who would've thought taking care of dogs could be so exhausting? Every two hours she ran up the stairs, took them out of their crate and down the back stairs. Of course they wanted to play besides doing their business, which took time she didn't have. What was she thinking, agreeing to a dog for Cody? This was only temporary, and she could barely handle it.

How would she handle Max once Holly left after Christmas? She couldn't just close up the shop every few hours, and she couldn't bring the dog into the store. She charged into the apartment.

The puppies yipped at her.

"Oh, I know. You need attention, don't you?" She opened the gate and clipped on their leashes. "Come on. If you go fast we can play a little." She led the dogs outside and in no time they were tugging her forward. "Okay. Just a short walk up the street and back, but we need to hurry." She allowed them to pull her along and investigate all the foreign smells their sniffers were picking up on. Too soon she had to turn them around and head back to the apartment.

The dogs whined when she closed the crate door.

"I know, little ones, but it won't be much longer. Be good." She quickly washed her hands and dashed down the stairs. "You miss me?"

Holly rolled her eyes. "Hardly. It's quiet today."

"I noticed. If I didn't need to step out to take care of the puppies I'd send you home. Of course the moment I did, this place would be hopping with customers."

Holly chuckled. "You're probably right. What you need is a dog walker."

"Hire someone to come and take them out for me?"

"Exactly."

"That's a great idea." Surely a dog walker wasn't too expensive. It had to be cheaper than paying Holly to stick around when things were slow.

"I have a friend who'd be perfect."

"Wonderful." Keira took the contact information. A smile tugged at her lips. She could do this. It just took a little planning, which Pete's spontaneous trip didn't allow. It had snowed pretty hard last night. She wished he'd at least called to let her know he'd made it safely across the pass. She worried her bottom lip.

"You all right?" Holly touched her arm.

"I'm just thinking about Pete. He was trying to beat the storm and left last night, but since it hit early he ended up in the middle of it." She shrugged. "I just worry. I wish he had waited until today to leave, or better yet, not gone."

"Sometimes it's hard not to worry, but no matter how hard we try to protect those we love, things happen that are out of our control."

The truth of the words slammed her gut. "That's pretty deep."

"Hey, don't make fun."

"I wasn't." Was all her caution for nothing? Holly's words made so much sense she was embarrassed to even think about all the times she'd avoided getting behind the wheel of a car. Not to mention being scared of allowing Cody to go out when the road conditions weren't ideal. Yet her fear was useless. There were some things she had no control over.

Holly spoke, pulling Keira from her thoughts. "I guess that's why the Bible talks about faith so much. We have to believe that God will take care of us and those we love. Even when bad things happen."

Suddenly Keira's stomach knotted and her throat thickened with unshed tears. She blinked rapidly. What was wrong with her? "I'm not feeling well, Holly." Her voice caught. "Will you lock up at six for me? I'm going to go upstairs to lie down."

"Of course. Do you need anything?"

"No, thanks. When Susan gets here with Cody, will you send them up?"

"Sure."

Keira nodded and slowly climbed the stairs. She almost never got sick and this had come on so fast. Maybe it was emotions making her feel ill. She opened the crate door for the dogs, then lay on the chaise. Holly's words echoed in her mind.

Faith.

Keira believed she had faith in God, but realized ever since Michael was killed she'd tried to control everything. Gradually the faith she'd placed in God had transferred to herself.

All the what-ifs of life bombarded her imagination. She squeezed her eyes shut as tears streamed down her cheeks. It was too much. She couldn't stop bad things from happening and she didn't have the energy to worry about the what-ifs anymore.

Her hands shook and she wrapped her arms around her stomach as sobs wracked her body. After a bit, the surge of tears dried up with a hiccup. Sniffing, she wiped her nose and tucked her arm under her head, exhaustion draining the energy from every muscle.

"Keira?" Gentle hands shook her awake.

"Susan." Keira sat up and looked around the room. "Where's Cody?"

"In his bedroom playing with the dogs."

"The dogs! What time is it? They didn't make a mess, did they?"

"Everything is fine. Cody and I took them out when we got here about thirty minutes ago. You've been sleeping for a while. Are you sick?" Susan felt her forehead. "You don't feel feverish."

"I'll be fine. Let's just say I had an awakening, and I'm not proud of myself. I don't know why I felt so awful. I'm much better now." But her stomach was queasy and all she wanted to do was sleep.

"What's this about, Keira? Holly told me that the two of you were talking and you turned white as a sheet and looked ready to get sick. It must be something pretty big."

"It's nothing I want to talk about right now."

"If you change your mind, call me. You know I'm a good listener."

"Okay."

"Promise?"

"Yes. I imagine you have someplace to be."

"No. Thought I'd make some soup and sandwiches for you and Cody and hang out here tonight."

Keira held in a groan. The last thing she wanted was Susan hovering.

"I'll take care of everything. You can take a nice hot bath, and I'll bring dinner to your room when you get out."

Being pampered sounded nice, but not necessary. "Thanks, but you don't need to do that. I'll be fine." She stood. "Look, I'm already feeling better. I just needed a little catnap."

Susan narrowed her eyes. "Your color does look good." She pushed up. "Well, if you're sure, I guess I'll head home."

"Thanks for taking Cody out this afternoon. He was so excited when Pete asked us to watch the dogs. I knew I'd never be able to contain him in the back room."

"No problem. He had fun making your Christmas present."

"He made me something?" When Susan wasn't working or socializing, she could usually be found in her art studio either painting or making pottery. She had quite a reputation around town with the locals, too. It wouldn't be much longer and she'd be able to quit her day job and open her own shop. Too bad the candy store wasn't larger or she'd share the space with her. Of course, Susan already owned her own CPA business, so she could display her work there if she wanted to.

Susan's eyes twinkled with the "I know something you don't know" gleam. "Remember I'm only a phone call away if you need anything."

"I know. Thanks again." Keira walked her friend to the door and let her out.

"Mom?" Cody stood in his bedroom doorway with Max cradled in his arms.

"Hmm?"

"When's Mr. Pete coming back?"

"I'm not sure. Why?"

"Just wondering. I like taking care of his dogs."

"I'm glad, sweetie."

The phone rang and she checked the caller ID. Her stomach flip-flopped.

Pete.

10

"How's the conference, Pete?" Keira held the phone to her ear as she leaned against the window frame and took in the Christmas scene outside. Wreaths adorned the lampposts and tiny snowflakes fell from the sky.

"Going well. I plan to head home Thursday. Is everything okay there? The dogs doing well?"

"Just fine. Don't worry about Max and Molly." She couldn't help the smile that touched her lips at his protective attitude toward the puppies.

"I was only partially talking about the dogs. I was thinking of you and Cody, too."

"You were?" She heard the surprise in her voice. Pete had never expressed concern for their well-being. "I have a touch of something, but I'm fine. Cody's thrilled to have the puppies here."

"Maybe I should come back sooner if you're not feeling well. I don't have to stay for the whole thing."

Keira chuckled. "Relax, Pete. I'm fine, and the dogs

are in good hands. We'll see you when you return."

"If you're sure."

"I am. Thanks for the call." She hung up and caught her reflection in the window. Large sad eyes stared back at her. "Knock it off, Keira." She had to stop this melancholy. It wasn't healthy and there was no reason for it. Except she couldn't escape the feeling that haunted her earlier. The word *trust* nagged her. Hmm. Seemed like faith and trust were synonymous.

She wanted to trust God, but it was so hard. Clearly bad things happened even on God's watch, or Michael wouldn't be dead. But it seemed God was trying to get her attention and He'd done a good job of it. A verse she'd memorized as a child popped into her mind.

The Lord is good, a refuge in times of trouble. He cares for those who trust Him... Nahum 1:7.

She should try harder to let go of her fear. Driving was out of the question, but perhaps she'd let Susan take her to church this Sunday. After all, it was less than a mile away. Baby steps.

"Mom?" Cody tugged on the hem of her shirt.

She started. "I didn't see you there. What do you need?"

"I'm hungry."

Keira sighed and moved to the kitchen. Maybe she should've taken Susan up on her offer to make dinner. Before long, scrambled eggs sizzled in a pan. She warmed a tortilla shell sprinkled with cheese and placed a scoop of eggs on top. "Here you go, Cody. One scrambled-egg burrito."

"Yum!" He gingerly carried the plate to the table and climbed onto the chair.

She stacked her plate with food and joined him. "Did you have fun with Aunt Susan today?"

"Yep." He stuffed his mouth.

"What'd you do?"

"Nothing much." He said with a full mouth.

"Don't talk when you're chewing."

His frown puckered his little brows and his lips pouted. "You asked a question."

She hid a smile behind her napkin. He had a point. She looked to where the puppies snuggled on their bed, snoring. "Those are a couple of really cute dogs. Don't you think?"

Cody nodded this time, then swallowed. "Aunt Susan helped me write my Christmas list, and I asked for a puppy. Do you think I'll get one?"

Keira shrugged. "Guess you'll have to wait and see."

"I can't wait."

She chuckled. "Seems to me you don't have much choice, buddy. Besides, Christmas is only another week and a half away."

He groaned. "That's so long!"

"Well, at least we get to take care of the dogs. Plus, you play with them almost every day. That's pretty nice, right?"

"Yeah. I like Mr. Pete."

"Me, too." She wiped her mouth on a napkin and set

it aside. "If you're finished, how about you take a bath? I'll be right there to pour the bubbles." She quickly cleared the table, then found Cody dumping bubble bath into the tub. "Whoa, there. I think that's enough. What happened to waiting for me?"

"I like lots of bubbles, Mom." His brows puckered.

She laughed, scooped up a handful of suds and deposited them on his nose. "I can see that."

Cody sank down into the tub and played with his water toys. Keira leaned against the wall and wondered what it would be like to have a man in the house again to share these special moments with.

Keira bundled Cody in his winter wear and nudged him toward the door. "Come on, I have to open the store at ten, and if you want to play in the snow with the dogs we need to move."

"Okay." Cody ran out the front door that led to the candy store.

She'd decided it'd be a safer choice considering the fresh snow that'd fallen overnight. They stepped outside and frigid air smacked her in the face. "Brrr. Good thing the puppies have coats, or they might freeze."

Cody took her hand. "When will Mr. Pete be back?"

"This afternoon. He'll pick up Molly and Max on his way home."

Cody's shoulders slumped, and he dragged his booted feet through the snow. "I wish we could keep them."

"I know." She looked toward the deserted park.

"Seems like you have the run of the place today." Since it was only eight-thirty in the morning, few people were out. Just the way she liked it. The quiet hush pulsated in her ears, the silence broken only by an occasional car.

They crossed the street and moved into the open space. Keira released the dogs and laughed as they romped with Cody. Max dug his nose into the snow. He jerked his head up, ears alert and a mound of powder stuck to his snout. "Oh, Max. Really?" She reached down and rubbed the snow off. The silly puppy did it again only this time he sneezed, then charged at Molly.

Cody busily worked on a stockpile of snowballs. "What'cha doing?"

"Making a stash, for when all the kids get here."

"Sweetie, I don't think we're going to see any other kids this morning. It's too early."

He shrugged, and instead of pouting like she expected, he tossed a snowball in the air toward the puppies, who leaped for them. Keira laughed and formed a ball to toss. Who would've thought it'd be so simple to entertain puppies?

Thirty minutes later, wet and cold, they hurried home to warm up.

"Mom?"

"Hmm?" Keira set a mug of hot cocoa in front of Cody, then sat beside him.

"Can I have a friend over?"

"That's a great idea, but not while I'm working."

"You're always working," he whined.

Keira pursed her lips. She'd known this day would come, but hadn't expected it at age four. Maybe it was time to find permanent help with the store. Until recently Cody had been happy to play by himself, but his discontent with that arrangement had become clear. "I'll tell you what. Once Christmas is over I'll hire someone to work one day a week and that will be our special day to do whatever we want."

"Like have a friend over?" Excitement lit his eyes.

"Yep, or we could go exploring, or whatever we want."

"What about the other days?"

She couldn't afford to pay someone to work more than twenty hours a week, but Cody did have a point. She needed to cut back on her nearly sixty-hour week. Besides running the store, she had orders to send and paperwork to deal with. The list went on, but she didn't want to think about it. "Good question. I'll see what I can do. Fair enough?"

He nodded.

She ruffled his hair and placed a soft kiss on his forehead. "Good. Now go brush your teeth. We need to get downstairs."

Another thought struck her: if she freed up a couple days a week, that would give her a little time to work on the trust issue God had been challenging her with. A grin touched her lips. And it'd free up some time for a social life. Now, that was something to look forward to.

Pete sat across from Keira at Starbucks. "So Cody really took you to task, huh?" The subtle blush on her cheeks brought a smile to his lips.

She chuckled. "I suppose so. I promised I'd hire someone after Christmas, but then decided to look right away. My hours are ridiculous and now that Cody's nearly five, I needed to make a few changes in how I run my business." She took a sip of her mocha. "Anyway, I was thrilled to find a woman who's been a stay-at-home mom for the past twenty years. Before she took time out to raise her children she managed a fast-food restaurant in Wenatchee. I really like her and think she'll be a good fit for the shop."

"I hope she works out."

"Me, too. Oh, and the best part is she's willing to work Sundays and Mondays, so I'll have two days off in a row."

"That's great!" Maybe now Keira would have time for a little fun. He sure hoped she'd spend some of that free time with him. He'd made a decision while at the conference. It was time to stop looking at the past and live in the present. Most important, it was time to trust. It wouldn't always be easy, but with God's help he believed it was possible to move past his hurt and learn to trust again.

Keira touched his hand, her expression suddenly serious. "Everything okay? You looked lost for a minute."

"Just thinking." Pete focused on her delicate fingers

and soft skin and resisted the urge to run his thumb along it. He'd bide his time. Soon enough he'd be able to hold her without making things awkward between them. After all, they couldn't ballroom dance without some contact.

"So, what are you thinking about?" Keira grinned. "You have a gleam in your eye that suggests mischief."

"Who, me?" He used his most innocent voice.

Keira laughed and pushed away from the table. "I'd better get to the store. It's almost time for Holly's break. She's closing tonight so I can get off early."

The ball started at seven. How much time did a woman need to get ready? Thinking about his high school days he remembered it'd taken his sister half the day to get ready for the prom between hair, makeup and nails. He offered his arm and Keira slipped her hand through it.

"Thanks. What time will you be by tonight?"

"Six forty-five."

"I hate to ask, but my dress is rather poufy and long. How exactly are we getting to the Festhalle?"

"It's a surprise, but don't worry, your dress will be safe. Do you want me to come up the back stairs?"

"No way. I'd never make it down those in one piece. I'll watch for you from inside the store."

"Sounds like a plan." He guided them across the street and stopped in front of the candy shop. With her jacket zipped to her chin and a red scarf bundled around her neck, she looked adorable. He took her hands and drew her close, then wrapped her in a hug. "See you later."

She looked up at him. The question in her beautiful

eyes warmed him from head to toe. Her lips parted. "I'm looking forward to it."

He released her and stepped back.

A serene smile covered her face. "Thanks for asking me to the ball, Pete. I'm sure there are other things you'd rather be doing. Not many men enjoy that kind of thing."

"Sounds like fun to me. No need to make me out the hero."

"You're my hero," she said in a whisper, then fled inside without looking back.

His stomach did a strange lurch. He watched her through the window for a moment longer, then turned *away*. Keira Noble, I don't know how you did it, but you opened my heart to the possibility of love again.

Keira stepped into the red gown and stared at the mirror. Too bad she didn't have long enough hair for an updo. Pretty rhinestone barrettes would have to do. She slipped into silver-toned satin pumps and glided into the main room of her apartment with a twirl. "Well?"

"You look pretty, Momma."

"Thanks." She felt pretty, too. "Aunt Susan should be here soon."

He nodded and continued to work on the ship he was building. "Can I stay up until you get home?"

"Sorry, kiddo. I'll be very late."

A knock sounded on the door and her son ran to open it. Susan walked in. "Wow. You look amazing. Pete isn't going to know what hit him."

"Thanks. You don't think it's too much?"

Susan shook her head. "It's perfect. And the hair clips are just right. I don't know what you're worried about." Keira grabbed her clutch. "Thanks for watching Cody. Did you bring stuff to spend the night?"

"Nope. I sleep much better in my own bed, even if it's for only half the night." She giggled. "Be a good girl and come home by midnight, or your ride might turn into a pumpkin."

Keira laughed. "Yes, Mother." She draped a silver cape over her shoulders, then took the stairs down to the candy store and waited by the window. There weren't many people out since most of the stores closed early, but from her vantage point the village looked like a scene from a sparkly snow globe.

A horse-drawn carriage pulled up in front of her store and stopped. *That's odd. It doesn't normally come down this far.* She watched as a man wearing a black tux stood and stepped out. Her breath caught in her throat—Pete. She pushed open the door and walked outside.

He bowed and lifted his hand, palm out. "Your carriage awaits, milady."

Too awestruck to reply, she rested her hand in his and climbed into the beautiful carriage. He followed and sat across from her. For the first time she regretted the enormous ball-style skirt that took up the entire bench seat.

"You look beautiful." Pete's smile matched his

words.

"Thanks, so do you." She shook her head. "I mean, you look handsome."

He chuckled. "Good thing we're not going far or you'd freeze." He held up the blanket beside him. "You want this?"

As tempting as the offer was, she didn't want to risk marring her dress. "No, thanks. Like you said, it's not far."

Keira scooted her full dress off the other half of the seat. "You can sit here." She tried to keep her teeth from chattering.

"The view is better from this side." Pete winked. "But if you insist." He shifted to the space beside her.

Her face heated and probably matched the color of her dress. "This is amazing. I can't believe you went to all this trouble."

"Why not?"

"I don't know." She grinned and savored the priceless moment. There was no point in overanalyzing the gesture. A few pedestrians gawked and waved. Giggling, she did the parade wave—elbow-elbow, wrist-wrist. "This is too much fun." The village lights glistened off the snow, creating a magical world as the clip-clop of horse hooves pulled them slowly toward the end of the long street to the Festhalle.

Pete stepped out and offered her a hand down. "You ready for this?"

"I think so. Any word on what the surprise part is all about?"

"Nope. But we're about to find out."

He opened the ornate wooden door and handed over their tickets.

Several couples mingled in the foyer. Pete guided them to the double doors leading into the main room.

Keira caught her breath. "This is lovely." Twinkle lights outlined the room and lit snowflakes hung from the ceiling. A Christmas tree adorned with hundreds of lights and oversized red-and-purple ornaments sat in the center of the large room. "Do you see anything that would indicate what the surprise is?"

"No. But I agree it's an amazing transformation."

The Festhalle had never looked so beautiful, at least when she'd been there. A string ensemble serenaded the dancers with a waltz. Women in evening dresses glided on the arms of men sporting black tuxedos.

"Would you like to dance?" Pete held out his hand.

"Of course, but I have to warn you. I'm not very good."

He chuckled. "That makes two of us. Hopefully we won't leave with bruised feet."

"With the size of the skirt on this dress, there's no way that'll happen. You won't get near my feet."

He took her hand and rested his other hand on her back. "Let's see if I can remember how this is done."

"Same here." Keira tried to focus on the steps, but knew she was failing and probably would've taken a nosedive were it not for Pete's strong arms holding her tight.

"What's wrong?"

Her attention focused on Pete's face. "What do you mean? Did I miss a step?"

He smiled and his gaze softened. "No, but you look disturbed about something."

"I'm feeling a little conspicuous. I thought, since it's an old-fashioned ball, the women would dress accordingly."

"Well, I, for one, think you look amazing, and I'm glad you went the traditional route. Otherwise we'd both probably end up with broken toes."

She chuckled. "Thanks. Where are the puppies tonight?"

"At the clinic. They spend so much time there I figured they'd be content. Plus, Dr. Young is working late tonight. Just before closing, a cat came in needing special attention."

"That's what I call commitment."

"Yeah. I suppose, but it worked out well for me." He twirled them in a wide circle, then came to a stop when the song changed. "Would you like something to drink? I noticed refreshments in the foyer."

"Water sounds wonderful." She wound her fingers through his and strolled beside him. "Thanks for asking me to come tonight. I think I'd have left already if I'd been alone." She noticed many couples and only one or two singles around the room.

"You're welcome. Thanks for saying yes." He handed her a water bottle and took one for himself. "Were you worried?" she asked.

"I'm always a little off when I'm with you."

Her brow puckered. "Why?"

He shrugged. "Guess you throw me off balance." He winked. "You ready to go back in?"

"Sure." Strains from a waltz that reminded her of the songs a merry-go-round played filtered through the air. She rested her hand on Pete's forearm. "I'm concerned that I've said or done something that makes you feel awkward around me."

"Just the opposite. It's me who said something and now I regret it."

She moved along with the people streaming into the Festhalle. "Please tell me what it is."

He took a deep breath and let it out in a puff. "It's the whole thing about not dating single moms. Something is changing inside me, Keira."

Keira's stomach fluttered. "What are you saying?"

He frowned and shook his head. "I'm saying I like you. A lot." He flashed a grin, clearly trying to diffuse the tense sparks between them.

Keira ignored the knot in the pit of her stomach. Was he willing to consider a relationship with her after all? Movement on the stage distracted her. "Oh, look." She pointed to the councilwoman with a microphone.

"Welcome to Leavenworth's first Christmas Ball. I hope you're enjoying yourselves." Applause broke out. She gestured, quieting the crowd. "Thank you. Now, I know many of you are wondering why this is called the

Christmas *Surprise* Ball."

Movement in the room stilled and every face lifted in an expectant hush.

"A few years ago our community began raising funds for an ice-skating rink. Several other community leaders and I have organized this special event to thank you all for your hard work and dedication. I'm pleased to announce the goal has been met and we will break ground as soon as it thaws."

Whoops and whistles erupted. Of course. Now the guest list made sense. They were all store owners and community members who'd taken part in fund-raising.

Pete spoke into Keira's ear. "Does Cody ice skate?"

"Not yet, but I imagine he'll be a fan. Isn't this exciting? Can you imagine how busy the rink will be?"

He shook his head and a grin lit his eyes. "In this town? Yes."

The musicians struck up a soft rendition of "Silver Bells." Pete took her into his arms and swayed to the music.

Two hours later Pete whispered into her ear, "Are you ready to leave?"

Keira sighed, not ready for the night to end. "Yes. I suppose everyone will be heading out soon."

"The carriage should be waiting to take us back."

He led her outside and helped her up.

A moment later they clip-clopped away. He draped his arm on the seat behind Keira, softly rubbing her shoulder. "I had fun tonight."

"Me, too." She rested her head on his chest. If only she could make this night last forever.

The carriage rolled to a stop. Pete climbed down and helped her out. He shook the driver's hand. "Appreciate the ride."

The driver nodded and the carriage rolled away.

"You're not riding anymore?"

"No. I'll walk to the clinic. I always leave my SUV there." He guided her toward the shelter of the storefront.

"Would you like to go inside where it's warm?" Keira didn't want the evening to end.

"I should be going. Besides, didn't you say Susan's watching Cody?"

"Yeah. I suppose you're right." She stepped up on tiptoe and placed a kiss on his cheek. "Thanks for making me feel like a princess."

"My pleasure." He drew her to his chest and dropped a soft kiss on her forehead. "Sleep well, Princess Keira."

Mesmerized, her eyes found his, which slid down to her mouth. He tilted his head and captured her lips. Her insides exploded like the finale of a fireworks display. Never had she felt so cherished.

Keira slipped into her apartment, then tiptoed past the couch where Susan slept.

"How'd it go?" Susan's husky voice shattered the quiet. Keira slapped a hand to her mouth to stifle a scream. "I thought you were sleeping."

Susan sat up and stretched. "I was, but I'm a light sleeper."

"It was fun. Let me change, and I'll be right back." Keira hustled into her bedroom and quickly got into pajamas, then pulled on a thick pair of extra-soft socks. After grabbing a blanket and tossing it around her shoulders, she tiptoed out to where Susan waited.

Susan curled her legs up in the corner of the couch, making room for Keira. "You took forever changing. I'm dying to know how tonight went."

"I was gone less than five minutes."

Susan let out an impatient sigh. "Come on, already. When you left earlier I saw the carriage from the window, and I've been imagining your date all night."

"It wasn't a date. Just two friends traveling together to the same place." Ha, who was she trying to kid? That was most definitely a date and as dates go it rated at the top. Especially the kiss.

"Yeah, right." Susan drew her from her thoughts. "He rented the horse and carriage. If that wasn't a date, then I'm not a twenty-seven-year-old spinster."

Keira giggled. "No way are you a spinster. Besides, who uses that word anymore?"

"I do. Now tell me about tonight."

Keira closed her eyes and envisioned the ballroom. "The Festhalle looked amazing. There were white twinkling lights all over and a beautiful Christmas tree in the center of the room. Poinsettias decorated the stage where the instrumentalists played." She sighed. "It was like a dream." She didn't mention the kiss. That was between her and Pete, the perfect ending to a wonderful evening.

"Sounds nice. And from the look on your face, I'd say you had fun."

"Oh, yeah."

"Were there lots of people there?"

"Yes, but not uncomfortably so. Oh, and guess what the surprise was?" She rushed on without giving Susan time to respond. "We have enough funds to start the ice skating rink!"

"That's great news. Will there be a Christmas Ball next year?"

Keira shrugged. "Beats me, but I doubt it. I think this was a one-time deal because of the ice rink. A sort of thank-you to community leaders and volunteers for all their effort."

"Well, I'm glad you went."

"Me, too. I'm sorry you missed it."

"Don't be. I watched a movie and fell asleep early. It was a nice evening and Cody was a sweetie."

"Good." Keira yawned. "I thought I'd be up all night, but I'm wiped out. You may as well go back to sleep. I hate for you to be heading home so late."

"This couch is pretty comfy. Think I will." She pulled the blanket up to her chin and rested her head back. "'Night."

"See you in the morning." Keira stood and tiptoed to her room. Pete had promised not to kiss her, yet he had anyway. She hoped it meant they'd gone past just friendship, but maybe he didn't take kisses as seriously as she did. Ugh. She had to stop thinking about it.

11

Pete hummed "Jingle Bells" as he buttoned his shirt. The puppies wrestled nearby, and the aroma of fresh coffee filled his house. He had the day free to do whatever he wanted and with Christmas less than a week away, a little shopping was in order. At the top of his list was chocolate. Sure, it'd probably be better to buy it after church tomorrow, but he wanted an excuse to see Keira today.

The memory of their kiss lingered at the front of his thoughts and he wouldn't mind repeating it. He shaved and splashed on a little aftershave, then whistled for Max and Molly. "Let's go." The puppies raced for the door. He grabbed his wallet and stuffed it into his back pocket, then shrugged into his wool coat and wrapped a black scarf around his neck. Finally he grabbed the travel mug from the counter. A day without coffee would be like a day without air—he wouldn't survive.

Fifteen minutes later he strode into Keira's candy shop. To his surprise, she wasn't there. Holly stood behind the counter with a woman he hadn't seen before. He spoke softly to Holly. "Where's Keira?"

"She's taking the day off."

"Is that normal?" He frowned, unable to remember her not running the store. Sure, she'd mentioned hiring someone new, but he'd thought that would begin after Christmas.

"It's the new normal. Actually she has Sundays and Mondays off now, but asked Lily to come in an extra day this week. Apparently she got in late last night and, with Christmas only a few days away, needed time to get ready."

Pete hid a grin. "Okay. Thanks."

"She mentioned you'd be stopping by sometime in the next few days to pick up an order. Did you want to get that now?"

"No. I'll come back Tuesday." He turned to leave.

"You know…"

Holly's voice stopped him and he turned back.

"You could call her or even knock on her door. You don't need to wait for Tuesday." She flashed a mischievous smile and wiggled her brows.

His face had to be the color of the poinsettia on the counter. "Right. Bye." He fled the shop and walked the nearest coffee shop. After ordering a peppermint mocha, he pulled out his cell phone. Keira picked up on the second ring.

"Hi, Pete. What's up?"

"Not much. I'm over at the coffee shop across the

way from you and thought if you weren't busy you and Cody might like to join me."

The long pause unnerved him. "Hello?"

"I'm here. Sorry. We were just getting ready to go out and build a snowman. But we'll head your direction first. Be right there."

Less than five minutes later Keira and Cody bolted through the doorway. When Cody saw him, he grinned wide and waved with a mitten-covered hand. He said something to his mom, then rushed over to the table.

"Hi, Mr. Pete. Mom's getting me a hot chocolate and then we're going to build a snowman."

"That's what I heard. Seems to me you'll need another hot cocoa when you're finished. Playing in the snow is cold work."

Cody nodded. "I know." The gleam in his eyes suggested the child was already scheming for another treat.

Keira placed a cup in front of Cody and sat beside him. "What are you doing today, Pete? Want to help us build a giant snowman?"

"I could probably squeeze you into my schedule." He teased. He looked to Cody. "Max and Molly are in my SUV. When we're done here we can go get them."

Cody gulped his drink and set the cup down with a thump. "I'm ready!" He pulled on Keira's arm. "Let's go, Mom. Max and Molly will freeze in Mr. Pete's car."

Pete chuckled and placed a hand on Cody's shoulder. "Relax. They're resting on their snuggly bed, and they keep each other warm."

Cody looked like he might argue, but instead crossed his arms and sent his mother a look Pete couldn't read.

"Holly tells me your schedule changed."

"Yes. I moved up the timetable for the new hire. Cody has big plans for my days off."

"Yep. Tomorrow me and Mom are skiing and snow-tubing. Then we're going to have a snowball fight."

"And after that I'll collapse on the couch for a whole day."

"And I get to have a friend over to play!" Cody said.

Keira took a sip from her cup. "What about you? When are your days off?"

"Weekends, but I'm on call every other."

"If you're free after church tomorrow you're welcome to join us."

What about her fear of driving in the snow? "Who are you, and what have you done with Keira?"

Cody busted up laughing. "She is Momma, silly."

Pete thumbed his chin. "Hmm. She does look like your mom, and her voice is the same."

"That's because she *is* my mom." Cody shook his head and looked at him like he'd grown elephant ears.

"Well, if you say so," he said with a straight face, then grinned wide. "You know I'm just playing, right?"

Cody shrugged.

Clearly the child had fallen for his tease. "How about we go build that snowman?"

Cody jumped up. "Yay!" He tugged on Keira's arm.

"Let's go. Mom. This is going to be the best snowman ever."

Pete caught Keira's gaze and held it for a moment. Her eyes filled with questions, but he ignored them, unsure himself what was happening between them.

She broke eye contact and stood. "I thought we'd head to the park along the river."

"Okay." He wondered why they would go down that steep hill when there was a perfectly good play area a few hundred feet away, but kept his thought to himself. "I'm parked nearby, so it'll only take a minute to get the dogs."

He strode for his 4Runner and put the puppies' coats and leashes on in no time.

Keira grasped Cody's hand and ambled beside him. "How are you planning to get to Ski Hill tomorrow?"

"The roads are pretty clear, so I asked my father-in-law to give us a lift."

"Will you be able to handle it?"

"I'm going to try. God's been dealing with me on trusting Him, so I figured since Cody talked me into cutting back my hours it was about time I conquer this fear."

"But you're not driving."

"Baby steps, Pete. Baby steps."

He grasped her hand and gave it a gentle squeeze. "I'm proud of you. From what I understand, this is a big deal."

"The biggest."

They rounded the corner to the park and Cody pulled

free from his mom.

"Stay off the bridge! I don't want to fish you out of the water."

"Okay!" He altered his course and instead ran left toward the open space where plays were performed in the summer.

Pete held on to the dogs' leashes, unwilling to risk their curiosity in an unfamiliar place. "Your son is a tornado of energy."

"Tell me about it." They strolled toward where Cody had begun the base of the snowman.

"I've been meaning to try out Ski Hill. Maybe I could take you and Cody there tomorrow?"

Keira grinned. "I'd like that."

"Your father-in-law won't mind?"

"Not at all. In fact I think he'll be pleased, but I'll warn you now. People will talk."

"What do you mean?"

"Us. First we were seen together at the ball last night, then the coffee shop this morning and Ski Hill tomorrow. Before you know it they'll have us engaged."

Pete laughed. "True."

A snowball struck Keira in the stomach and a scream escaped her lips.

Pete laughed. "Guess you didn't see that coming." A snowball broke against his chest. "This is war, little man."

He reached down and scooped a handful of powder and formed it into a ball, then sent it soaring toward Cody. Her son twisted and it smacked into his back.

Keira sighed. She'd never enjoyed snowball fights, but like they say, if you can't beat them, join them. She dropped to her knees and formed several balls as fast as she could. Streams of sunlight blinded her view of Cody until he tore across the park. She fingered a large snowball and tossed it toward him.

"You need to work on your aim, Keira." Pete sent one flying toward Cody. It splattered on the boy's shoulder. Puffs of steam blew from Cody's mouth as he giggled.

A few minutes later Cody waved his arms above his head. "Let's finish the snowman now."

Keira gave Pete a high five. "Nicely done!" She brushed the excess powder off her clothes and gloves. "You ready to build this thing?"

The gleam in his eye said it all. Seemed Pete had tapped into his inner child. He bent down and formed a ball, then started rolling it in the snow, packing it as he moved closer to Cody. "How big should we make it?"

Her son stood on tiptoe and raised his arms as high as he could reach. "This high."

In no time, they'd created a respectable snowman. Keira stood back and admired their work.

"He needs a face." Cody reached into his jacket pocket and pulled out large black buttons.

Keira took a bag from her pocket containing licorice for the mouth.

Pete lifted Cody up so he could create the face.

"It's perfect." Cody clapped his hands and grinned wide. "Thanks, Mom and Mr. Pete. This was fun."

"I'm glad. Time for a picture. I wish I'd brought my camera, but this old thing will have to do." She pulled out her cell phone and held it up.

"Use mine." Pete handed her his phone.

"Thanks. How about you stand by the snowman with Cody? Then I'll get one of just Cody." Keira clicked off a few shots and handed the phone back to Pete.

Pete stuffed the phone in his jacket pocket. "I'll send the pictures to you later when my fingers aren't so cold."

For the first time in forever she felt like Supermom. Her stomach rumbled loud enough for everyone to hear.

"Hungry?" Pete raised a brow.

"I could eat. Want to come up to our place for a sandwich?"

"Sounds good to me."

They tromped along the snow-covered path to the main sidewalk and made their way up the steep hill toward her apartment. Keira knew her face had to be glowing. She hadn't had this much fun since she was a kid. Pete's playful side surprised and delighted her.

"You sure you're up to another day of play tomorrow?"

Pete nodded. "I wouldn't miss it."

Sunday morning Keira excused Cody from the table and sipped her coffee. Susan sat across from her with a worried look on her face.

"Are you sure about this, Keira? It snowed last night and the roads are a little slick."

Keira set the cup down and it clattered against the table. "My hands are shaking so bad I couldn't even put on eyeliner today, but I'm determined that Cody and I will ride with you to church, and then this afternoon we're going to Ski Hill with Pete."

"I heard you had coffee together yesterday. Is there something you'd like to share?" Susan quirked a brow.

"Not yet." She may not understand what was happening between them, but one thing was certain, she'd grown to care for Pete in a very short time.

"At least tell me if he's gotten over his issue with dating you."

"That's just it." Keira shrugged. "I don't know for sure."

"Sounds like the two of you need to have a heart-to-heart."

Keira pressed her lips together. She'd tried that once before and hadn't liked his answer, but things had changed. He'd kissed her, even if he still claimed they were friends. If she took Susan's advice she'd be putting it all on the line. "He's admitted that he really likes me, but what if he hasn't changed his mind?" She spoke barely above a whisper. She'd humiliate herself and probably be embarrassed to ever speak to him again. Oh, why did she feel like an insecure teen girl? She was a grown woman. It wasn't like she'd never been in love before. Her eyes widened and her heart pounded. Her breathing came in short bursts.

Susan's troubled eyes found hers. "Hey, you okay?"

Keira nodded. "Just freaking myself out." Could it really be true? Impossible. But no, she loved him, or at least she thought she did. When had that happened?

Susan reached across the table and placed her hand over Keira's. "Is this about riding to church or Pete?"

"Both, I guess, but more Pete." Keira took slow deep breaths.

"Wouldn't you rather know now before your heart's involved?"

"Too late." The pounding in her chest proved her words. She'd fallen for Pete.

Susan squeezed her hand before releasing it and pushed back from the table. "If you're serious about riding with me to church, then you'd better get ready."

"Okay." Keira stood. She didn't want to think about Pete anymore. On top of facing her biggest fear today, she was terrified Pete still wanted to be only friends. She blew out a puff of air—no more thinking. "I'll be right back. Cody's too quiet."

Sure enough, the mischief-maker had decided to fill the bathroom sink with water and placed several toys in it. Water soaked his sleeves up to his forearms. "Cody, what are you doing? You know we need to leave for church soon."

"Just playing." Her son held out a windup duck. "See." The duck zoomed across the sink and crashed into the other side.

"Yes, and I also see that you need to change your shirt. Go quick, while I clean this up."

Ten minutes later they tromped down the stairs to Susan's car.

"You're sure about this?" Susan asked as she opened the driver's door.

"Yes." *No!* After securing Cody in his booster seat, she clicked on her own seat belt, pulling it as tight as possible. *Does this thing have air bags?* She looked over her shoulder and noticed it had curtain bags as well as side and front-impact bags. At least there was one thing to be thankful for. Michael had been driving an older-model pickup without air bags. If it'd had them he might still be alive.

Susan put the car in reverse and backed out.

A jolt jostled Keira in her seat and sent shivers up her spine. She caught her breath. "What was that?" She gripped the windowsill with her fingers.

"Just a clump of snow."

"Oh." Keira closed her eyes, took a deep breath and let it out slowly. *Think happy thoughts.* At least the church was close. The car rolled forward and Susan pulled out onto the road. This wasn't so bad, much better than the parking lot. Keira opened her eyes. A car came near them and she squeezed her eyes shut. Who was she trying to kid? She was terrified out of her mind.

"Once I get onto the highway we'll be there before you know it."

"No rush," Keira squeaked. A few minutes later she

157

felt the car slow and turn, then slide. A whimper escaped her lips and she held her breath.

"Sorry about that. Hit a slippery spot when we pulled into the parking lot." Susan cast a worried look in her direction. "How're you doing?"

Keira took in a gulp of air. "Still alive."

Susan chuckled. "Always the drama queen."

"What's a drama queen?" Cody spoke for the first time since they'd gotten into the car. He must have sensed her stress. She'd always said he was a smart boy.

Susan looked in her rearview mirror. "A person who exaggerates things and makes something seem like a bigger deal than it is."

"And driving here today wasn't a big deal?" Keira asked.

"I suppose, but you added a dramatic flare," she said with a smile.

Susan parked and Keira scrambled out on shaky legs. She helped Cody. As she held his hand, they strolled into the church.

"Will Pete be in this service?" Susan asked.

"I don't think so. He usually goes to the later one."

"I thought he might come early since you're going skiing afterward."

"Beats me. Thanks for the ride." Keira excused herself to take Cody to his class and then washed her sweaty palms in the bathroom sink. The cold water soothed her frayed nerves. Maybe agreeing to ski *and* ride to church on the same day was too much. Walking home sounded like a good idea. At least she'd worn pants and boots.

Soft piano music washed over her as she entered the sanctuary. She found a spot near the middle and sat, thankful to have her feet planted on solid ground. Too soon the service was over and she made her way out of the sanctuary.

Susan nudged her shoulder. "Let me know when you're ready to go."

"I think the drive here was enough for one morning. Cody and I will walk home."

"You're sure?"

"Positive."

Susan gave her a quick hug. "I was proud of you this morning. I know how scared you were."

"Thanks. I'll catch you later."

12

Keira started when a knock sounded on her apartment door and checked her watch—eight-thirty. She set down the book she was reading and walked to the door. A look out the peephole showed Pete. Oh, no! She wore sweats and had her hair in a tiny ponytail at the back of her head. She quickly reached up and released her hair, allowing it to fall freely around her face.

Pete knocked again.

She unlocked and then opened the door. "This is a surprise. Come in."

He shook his head. "I can't stay long."

"That's fine, but it's cold out."

He stepped in and stood just inside the threshold. "Did you get my message this morning?"

"I did, but unfortunately I didn't think to check until you didn't show up."

He groaned. "I'm sorry. I can't believe I missed a day on the slopes for nothing."

"No worries. How's the other vet doing? You mentioned he had the flu."

"I haven't talked with him since his call this morning. I don't mind covering for him when I don't have plans, but—"

"Seriously, it's fine. Would you like some warm cider? It'll only take a minute to heat."

"Sounds good, but I should head home. I was only in town for a quick trip to get groceries. Do you think we could try skiing next weekend?"

"Sure. Cody is miffed at me for not going."

"I'm really sorry."

"Seriously, don't worry about it. After riding to church this morning with Susan, it'll take me all week to work up the courage to ride again." She shuddered.

"So the whole trusting God thing's a little tougher than you thought?"

She sighed. "I knew it'd be a struggle, but you gave me a reprieve, and I'm not one bit sorry. Cody and I had a nice relaxing day here, which we *never* do. He has a friend from church coming over to play tomorrow."

His shoulders sagged a little. "So no meeting in the park at noon?"

"Probably not. His buddy's coming for lunch, and then they're going to play. Are you sure I can't get you something?"

He reached for the door. "No, thanks. I'd better go."

"Well, if I don't see you sooner, have a Merry Christmas."

"Oh, you'll see me. I still need to pick up the chocolate I ordered for the clinic." He looked toward Cody's bedroom. "And I need to bring the *d-o-g* over, along with his supplies." He flashed a Hollywood grin and walked out.

How had she forgotten the puppy? Keira closed the door and leaned against it with a sigh. She'd never be able to sleep now. Thinking about Pete would keep her up for hours. At least Christmas was Thursday. She wondered if he realized that. He should've planned to pick up the candy he'd ordered for the vet clinic tomorrow. Hmm. That gave her an idea.

The following morning the sun shone bright in the cloudless sky. "Come on, Cody. Step it up. If you walk this slow all the way to the clinic we won't have time to play with the puppies before your buddy comes over." Cody sped up a bit, but not much. "I'm tired. Will you carry me?"

Keira sighed and scooped him up. "Just for a little bit. You're getting too big for me to carry you very far."

He wrapped his legs around her and tucked his head into her neck, snuggling close. She inhaled his sweet smell and held him tighter.

"Mom, can Mr. Pete come to Grandma and Grandpa's for Christmas with us? He's all alone and no one should be alone on Christmas."

"Sometimes I think you're too old to be four."

"Huh? I'm almost five."

Keira chuckled. "Never mind. I'll ask Grandma, and

if she says it's okay, then you may invite him. But you'll have to get down so I can call her real quick before we get to the clinic."

Cody walked beside her as she talked to Mary. "Okay, thanks. I'll let him know. Bye."

"What'd she say?"

"Yes."

"Yay! Do you think he'll bring the puppies?"

"You need to invite him first. And I don't want you to get upset if he says no. He may have plans we don't know about."

"Okay, but I hope he says yes. I want to play with the dogs on Christmas."

"You'll have plenty to play with."

Cody rattled on as if she hadn't spoken. "I also want to go sledding."

"That sounds like fun." They walked into the veterinary clinic parking lot. "Remember not to touch any of the pets without permission."

"Okay."

"And no sudden or loud noises. We don't want to scare the animals."

He nodded solemnly, his blue eyes serious.

They stepped inside and walked to the reception desk. Keira introduced herself and held up the bag with a box of chocolates inside. "I have a delivery for Dr. Harding. Is he available?"

The woman at the desk stood. "Let me check."

A minute later she returned. "He said to have you

wait in his office. Follow me."

Keira's heart pounded. What had she been thinking, coming here? He probably had a ton of patients to see and they'd be waiting forever. She should've just left the bag with the receptionist. Her thoughts were cut off when Pete hustled into the room.

"Is everything okay?" Concern etched his brows.

Keira stood and handed him the bag. "I thought you might like this now, since Christmas is only a few days away."

His brows relaxed and his face broke into a smile. "Thanks! You saved me a trip to the shop. I wish I could talk but I need to get back to work. May I call you tonight so we can talk about that other issue?" He glanced toward Cody.

"Of course."

Cody tugged on Pete's shirt. "Mr. Pete, can I see Max and Molly?"

"Sure. I'll have Meghan take you to them." He looked to Keira. "Thanks for this. I appreciate it."

Keira took Cody's hand and followed the woman to the kennels, trying to ignore her disappointment that Pete was too busy to visit.

"You two must be the reason Dr. Harding rushes off every day at lunch."

"He lets me play with Max and Molly."

"Well, here we are." A symphony of barking greeted them. The wall had kennels all around, but only five were occupied.

The puppies barked and pawed at the floor.

"Looks like they want to come out and play." Meghan opened the door and allowed the puppies to greet Cody.

Keira turned to Meghan. "Thanks. My son really missed these two."

Meghan laughed. "It looks like they missed him more." The dogs licked his face as if he were covered with doggie treats.

"Okay, you two. That's enough." Meghan put the animals back in the kennel. "I'll walk you out."

"I don't want to keep you from anything."

"I could use the break." She lowered her voice. "How's it going between you and Dr. Harding? When he had me book the carriage for the night of the ball, I knew you must be someone very special."

"Meghan, I need you in room two." Pete stood in the doorway.

"Be right there." She wiggled her fingers. "Ta-ta." Keira approached Pete. "I'm sorry. I didn't mean to get her into trouble."

"You didn't." He placed a peck on her lips, then turned and strode away.

Stunned, Keira touched her hand to her mouth. He'd kissed her in front of everyone!

Pete brushed past Meghan, who was gaping at him. Let her gawk. He grinned and almost laughed at the look of surprise on Keira's face. Well, there was more where that came from.

Until that moment he hadn't realized he was going to kiss her, but when she showed up today everything became clear. Keira was the woman for him regardless of anything else. Sure he'd been burned in the past, but he wasn't going to allow that to keep him from the woman he loved any longer.

Now to convince Keira he was the man for her.

Meghan sidled up beside him. "I like your girlfriend, and her little boy is adorable."

"She's not my girlfriend." But she would be if she'd give him a chance.

Meghan shrugged. "Whatever you say. But I think she likes you. Dr. Harding." She sashayed away.

With renewed determination, he attended to his patients. One way or another, he'd make his feelings known to Keira and the sooner the better.

Later that night, Pete sat on his couch with the puppies curled up on each side of him. He punched in Keira's number and listened to it ring.

"Hi, Pete."

"Hey. Sorry I couldn't talk earlier."

"No problem. I probably shouldn't have bothered you at work."

"Actually, I'm glad you did. I enjoyed seeing you. Both of you." He heard Cody's voice in the background.

"Pete, Cody wants to ask you something."

He heard the phone bang against something and

chuckled to himself

"Can you come to Grandma and Grandpa's house for Christmas with us? They said it's okay."

"Hmm. I don't know. Christmas is for families." His heart thrummed in his chest. Should he impose on a family gathering? He didn't want to hurt the child's feelings, but wasn't sure spending Christmas with Keira's in-laws was a great idea. Did they really want him?

"Please, Mr. Pete. You could bring Max and Molly and it'll be lots of fun."

He grinned. Now he saw where the little guy was going with the invite. He just wanted to be with the puppies. "How about you let me talk with your mom?"

"Okay."

"I'm sorry about that, Pete. If you have other plans or don't want to come, no worries."

"I'm sure he just wants to be with the puppies. Since he'll have Max it's a moot subject."

"I don't think so. He doesn't want you to be alone on Christmas. He told me so himself."

"Oh." Now what? Maybe this would be a good opportunity to show Keira how much he cared about her. But spending Christmas with her in-laws? "Can I ask you something?"

"Okay."

"Why aren't you spending Christmas with your own parents?"

"They couldn't come this year and, well, you know how I am about driving in the snow."

167

"You planning to walk to your in-laws'?"

"Well, no. But my parents live in Spokane and that's just too far for me to go."

"It's only a few hours if the roads are clear."

"Which they're not. Pete, what's wrong? Why are you avoiding the subject?"

"I guess I'm not crazy about intruding on your in-laws' Christmas, but I'd love to spend some of the day with you and Cody if it can be arranged."

"Really? I'd like that, too, and I know Cody would."

Over the next several minutes they schemed an idea that would make Cody's year. Pete had to admit, he was pretty excited himself.

Keira placed the phone on the battery charger and went into Cody's room to tuck him in.

"What did Mr. Pete say? Will he come with us?"

"I'm afraid not, sweetie."

Cody's little bottom lip protruded. "Why not? Doesn't he like us?"

"He likes us just fine, but he doesn't know Grandma and Grandpa and feels like he'd be uncomfortable at their house."

"Oh." He looked at her with wide eyes. "Won't he be sad all by himself?"

Keira's heart melted a little. She sat on the edge of her son's bed and pulled him into her arms. "You are a very sweet boy for caring so much about Mr. Pete. But he assured me that he has a wonderful plan for Christmas."

"Okay. I'm glad."

She kissed his forehead and tucked him under the sheets. "Love you. Good night."

"'Night, Momma."

Keira shut off the light and strolled out of his room. She had to have the most thoughtful child on the planet. Wouldn't he be surprised come Christmas morning? Her stomach fluttered in anticipation. This just might be the best Christmas yet. Then again, it could be the worst if she'd misread Pete.

The next morning, Keira flipped the sign to Open. Based on the orders she'd received, she braced herself for a wild day. Even before she could get behind the counter the door opened. She looked over her shoulder and her heart stuttered. "Pete. What are you doing here?"

"I needed some fresh air and wanted to run something by you. I know you're busy, but I had an idea, and I was hoping you'd join me."

"What'd you have in mind?"

"Night cross-country skiing out on my property."

She opened her mouth but no sound came out.

"Hear me out before you answer. It's supposed to be a clear evening. The stars and moon will light our way." Keira pursed her lips, but didn't want him to think she wasn't interested. "I'll see if Cody can spend the night with his grandparents." She didn't add that skiing on ungroomed trails sounded like a lot of work. Spending time with Pete would be worth it.

"We won't be too late. How about if we pick him up on our way back here?"

"That's nice of you to offer, but it'd be easier for them if he spent the night."

"Okay. Whatever works for you. I'll pick you up around six-thirty and have you home by eight." He spun on his heel with a light in his eyes and left.

Ugh. What had she gotten herself into? Not only would she freeze to death, she'd have to ride in a car.

Eight hours later Keira grabbed her ski jacket and put it by the door, along with her cross-country skis and boots. Business had been brisk today and she was tired, but not so tired she wouldn't enjoy being with Pete.

A knock drew her out of her thoughts. She opened the door. "Hi." She smiled up at Pete.

"You ready?"

"I think so."

He nodded toward her pile. "Want some help?"

"I'd love it." She handed him her skis, slipped on her jacket and grabbed her boots. "Let's go." She followed him down the stairs, the whole time taking deliberate deep breaths. Her heart raced at the thought of going for another car ride. But she'd agreed to this.

Pete slid her skis up the center of the 4Runner. "My place isn't far from here. I haven't been home yet, so I'll need a few minutes to get ready."

"Not a problem. Have you eaten?"

"No. You?"

"Didn't have time. I closed late."

"Let's pick up a burger on the way, then."

She nodded and got into the SUV, then folded her hands in her lap, willing them to stop shaking. *I can do this.* She had to be strong. She refused to humiliate herself in front of Pete.

Snores sounded in the backseat. Startled, Keira looked behind her and spotted Max and Molly. Pete must cart those two with him just about everywhere.

Pete got in beside her and started the engine. "All set?"

"Yep." Her voice confidently filled the SUV, but her insides screamed for her to jump out before it was too late. He'd backed in, so all he had to do was pull forward. Just like when she'd been in Susan's car, they bounced over several patches of compact ice and snow. She held her breath and squeezed her eyes shut.

A few minutes later Pete pulled off the road into a parking lot. "McDonald's okay?"

"Sure." The familiar scent of burgers and fries permeated his rig, and her muscles began to relax.

"How you doing?" Pete glanced at Keira. A moment ago, when she'd turned pale and had a death grip on the door, he'd thought she might pass out, but now she relaxed into the seat and breathed easily.

She shrugged. "How far to your place?"

"Ten minutes. Feel free to eat on the way." His eyebrows rose when she unwrapped her burger and a smile touched his lips. At least she was distracted from the road. "Thanks for this. I haven't eaten since breakfast."

"Why?"

"Holly bailed on me so I was on my own and had no time for food."

"That must be tough working in a candy shop. I think I'd have eaten half the stock."

She chuckled. "I enjoy a piece every now and then, but I seldom indulge."

Based on her trim figure he knew she told the truth. "Do you cross-country ski often?"

Keira shook her head and swallowed. "Not really. Michael and I used to, but until a week ago I never had the time and it didn't occur to me to go at night."

He turned onto the road that led to his house and Keira caught her breath. "You okay?" She had a white-knuckle grip on the door again and had stopped breathing. "Keira! What's wrong?"

She just shook her head.

He pulled off to the side, flipped on the dome light and took her face in his hands, forcing her to look into his eyes. "What's wrong, honey?"

A few tears dribbled out of the corner of her eyes. "It's this spot." She closed her eyes and shuddered. "This is the stretch of road where Michael was killed. I've avoided it since."

Pete sucked in a lungful of air and pulled her to his chest. Her body shook. He rubbed his hand in small circles on her back. "Do you want me to take you home?"

Keira sniffled and pulled away. "No. I want to do this. It's time."

"You sure?"

She nodded, but her eyes lacked conviction.

He gripped the wheel. "I'm turning back."

"No! I want to ski with you. Please, keep going."

A few minutes later he pulled into his driveway and parked. "Here we are. You sure you're okay?"

"I am, thanks."

He palmed her cheek. "I'm glad. Just give me a few minutes to scarf this food and change."

She opened the door and followed him inside. "Don't rush on my account."

He quickly fed the dogs and himself, then hustled to his bedroom and changed. He'd had no idea that bringing Keira out here would dredge up memories of her husband's accident, but she was making great progress overcoming her fear of winter driving.

Keira stood at the mantel, looking at a picture of Pete as a child with his family.

He cleared his throat. "Ready?"

She whirled around. "Is this you?" She held the photo in her hand.

He walked over and brushed his fingers against hers, taking the frame. "Yes."

"You were a cute kid."

"Thanks." He placed the frame back onto the mantel. "So, are we really going to go out into the freezing cold and do this?"

"Of course. And when we're finished I'll make you a steaming cup of hot chocolate and we'll warm up by the fire."

"Now *that* part of the plan I like."

He took her arm and led her back to the front door, where he slipped into his boots and grabbed his skis and poles. "Come on, you big baby. This is going to be so much fun, you'll be begging to come skiing with me every night."

"Ha. I doubt it, but I'm willing to give it a go at least once." She clipped her boots into the skis and held a pole in each hand.

"If you stay in my tracks it'll be easier for you."

"Good thinking."

He led the way, the soft swooshing of the skis and Keira's panting the only sound in the still night. He could do this for hours. "How're you doing?"

"Fine." The word came out in a short burst.

She didn't sound fine if the strain in her voice was an indicator. He slowed a little and looked over his shoulder. "There's a nice slope ahead, then we'll come to a dense patch of trees." He always enjoyed going downhill even if it was just a few feet.

The trees were the only negative about the route, but they'd be in and out of them in no time. He switched on the headlight he wore over his ski cap.

"Pete, I..."

He looked over his shoulder to see what the problem was. Her eyes widened.

"Look out!"

Something smacked him in the head. Pain seared through him and everything went black.

13

"Pete!" Keira dug in with the poles until she reached his side. She knelt beside him and touched his shoulder with her gloved hands. Blood streamed down the side of his face. "Wake up." Unshed tears burned her throat. Her chest tightened and her pulse raced. He'd hit a tree limb that left a gash in his forehead and knocked off his headlamp. Thank goodness the light was still working. She'd hate to be totally in the dark. She balled some clean snow and placed it on the wound, then patted his cheeks. No response.

"Pete Harding, don't you die on me!" She couldn't lose him. "Please wake up." She took a tissue from her pocket and wiped the blood away, then kissed his cheek and whispered, "You may not realize this, but you've changed my life. Before I met you I lived in a tiny world and now, because of you, I've started to live again. You can't die on me. I love you." Tears streamed down her face and she swiped at them. She held in a sob and took several deep breaths. Crying wouldn't do any good. Pete needed help. But she couldn't just leave him here.

She reached into her pocket for her cell phone, ripped off one glove and punched in 9-1-1. Nothing happened. She looked at the screen—no service.

Lord, what do I do?

She felt as if the Lord was telling her to trust Him.

Keira recognized that still, small voice and stood. "Pete, I'm going for help. Don't move."

"My head hurts," Pete moaned.

"You're awake!" She knelt beside him and cradled his hand in hers. "Where else do you hurt? Can you get up?"

"My leg." He winced. "My head feels like a bomb exploded inside."

"You probably have a concussion and need a few stitches. Any chance you can ski back to the house?"

"Doubtful. Snowmobile's in the garage. Key...kitchen drawer by the back door."

"I don't want to leave you alone." She looked over her shoulder toward where they'd come from and couldn't even see the house anymore.

"I'll be fine."

"Promise?"

"Hurry." His teeth chattered. "Freezing to death."

Her heart stuttered. "Don't say that!" She unzipped her jacket and laid it over his chest. It wasn't much, but it would help ward off the cold. "I'll hurry. Try to stay awake." She stood and glided back over the trail they'd made getting there, leaving the headlamp with Pete so she could find him again.

Fifteen minutes or so later she found Pete's house. The puppies raised their heads and let out a halfhearted yip, then promptly fell back to sleep.

Keira grabbed a clean dish towel and a blanket, then found the key in the drawer he'd mentioned and raced out to the garage. Minutes later she was flying across the snow on the snowmobile. Her hands tightened on the handlebars as the wind ripped through her shirt and burned her skin. She cut through the cold night air, teeth chattering. She'd always enjoyed snowmobiling, but not this time.

Pete's light shone ahead. She prayed she wasn't too late. Letting off the throttle, she came to a stop beside him.

She knelt in the snow. "How're you doing?"

He opened his eyes and grimaced. "Never better."

"Cute." She pressed the towel to his forehead. "Hold this here. We need to stop the bleeding."

He did as she said. That was a good sign. She stood and held out her hands. "I'll pull you up, then help you onto the snowmobile."

Pete grasped her hands and caught his breath when he started to rise. "Whoa. Hold on a sec." He squeezed his eyes closed.

"Come on, Pete. I know you're dizzy and in pain, but you need to get inside and warm up." She quickly retrieved her jacket and shrugged into it.

"Okay. I'm ready." His jaw tightened and he heaved to standing with her help.

Wrapping an arm around his waist, she helped him limp to the snowmobile. With care, Keira wrapped the blanket around his shoulders and tucked it tight around him so it wouldn't get tangled in any moving parts. She slid on in front of him. "Hang on." She felt his hands wrap around her middle and she hit the throttle, propelling them forward in the wrong direction down a short slope.

"Want me to drive?" Pete rested his head against her back.

"Think you can?"

"Nope."

"I didn't think so, either. Just hold on tight." She turned in the correct direction and maneuvered the sled up the slope and raced back to the house. She pulled up beside his SUV.

Pete let go and somehow managed to struggle to a standing position.

Keira helped him get into the passenger seat. "Where're your keys?"

He dug them out of his coat pocket and handed them over. "You know how to drive in snow, right?"

"Of course I know how. I just don't do it." She ran around to the driver's side and slid in. Her fingers gripped the steering wheel until they hurt.

"You need to turn the engine on or it won't move." His mouth curved in a half grin.

"Very funny." She inserted the key into the ignition and listened to the engine purr.

"You don't have to do this. We could—"

"No. Please be quiet, so I can get us to the medical center in one piece." She glanced over and noticed the cut on his forehead wasn't seeping blood through the towel anymore. One thing to be thankful for. "You're gonna be fine, Pete. The medical center isn't too far away."

"Why not go to Wenatchee? We're halfway there."

"We're just as close to Leavenworth and then I won't have to drive all the way home from Wenatchee." She backed up and pulled onto the road. Her palms sweated in her gloves. She used her teeth to pull off one, then the other.

"It's freezing in here. Why'd you take off your gloves?"

She had the heater on full blast but still heard Pete's teeth chattering.

"I'm roasting. Now shush. I need to concentrate." Did she dare tell him she was roasting because she was close to a panic attack? No, he'd probably insist on driving and then they'd both be doomed.

Focusing her attention forward, she pressed the gas pedal harder. "Hang in there, Pete. You'll be fixed up in no time."

Keira clamped her jaw tight, slowed and maneuvered around a bend, praying the tires would stay connected to the road. This was the turn Michael had lost control on, causing his pickup to flip. Her breathing became shallow and black spots danced before her eyes.

"How you doing?" Nervousness tinged Pete's voice. She shook her head and took a gulp of air. "You mind if I open a window?"

"Go ahead. I'll just turn the heater vents to face me. You're doing a good job, Keira."

The only stoplight in Leavenworth finally came into view. "We're almost there."

"I'm feeling a lot better now. I don't think I need to see a doctor."

"Too bad. You were unconscious for at least a minute." Although it felt like much longer, in truth it was probably less than a minute.

"I wasn't out that long, just in too much pain to talk. You didn't have to drive me here."

"How else would you have gotten help? You're in no shape to drive." He wasn't unconscious? Did that mean he'd heard what she'd said?

"You could've called an ambulance."

"I tried 9-1-1 on my cell—no service."

"I have a landline in my house."

Keira pulled into the parking lot. *Now* you tell me."

"I tried earlier, but you cut me off."

"Oh. I guess you're right." She opened the door and hustled around to the passenger side. "Okay. Take it nice and slow when you stand. No passing out allowed."

He chuckled. "No, that would not be a good. Once in a night is enough."

"Too much, if you ask me." She wrapped an arm around his waist and helped him limp inside.

They checked in and from there she was left alone while he was whisked away. At least the place wasn't busy.

She melted into the waiting room chair as the full impact of the night's events hit her. She'd driven in snow and survived! *And* she'd told Pete she loved him. Had he heard? Her cheeks burned at the thought.

Pete relaxed against the bed and mulled over Keira's words. Had he imagined her confession of love? Admittedly that tree limb had done a number on his head and he had the stitches to prove it.

Tonight hadn't gone the way he'd planned. He'd hoped for a romantic evening under the stars, followed by sipping hot chocolate in front of the fireplace. This was the night he was going to tell Keira how he felt about her and Cody. But thanks to a concussion, he'd earned a night in the hospital instead because he lived alone and the doctor insisted someone needed to keep an eye on him.

The dogs! He bolted up and winced. Better take it a little slower. The door whooshed open.

"Where are you going?" Keira stood in the doorway, a hand on her hip.

"Max and Molly need to be let out or I'll have a mess in my house."

"I'll call Josh. I'm sure he'll rescue them." She gently pushed him back until his head rested on the pillow.

"I'm fine. If you'll just give me a ride home..."

She bit her bottom lip. Something he noticed she did when nervous or uncomfortable. "If the doctor thought you should stay the night, then—"

"What does he know? There's nothing wrong with me except a slight concussion and a sprained knee. He's being overly cautious."

"Um, he's a *doctor.*"

"So am I. And I say I'm fine."

"You're a veterinarian, and I distinctly remember you telling me once that you didn't like to be addressed as Doctor because you're not a *real* doctor."

"Using my words against me—not fair."

"Maybe not, but true." She patted his shoulder. "Tell you what. I'll give Josh a quick call and if he can't get the puppies, then I'll drive over there myself and pick them up."

"You'd do that?" He took her hand. "I know I've said it before, but who are you and what have you done with Keira Noble? The Keira I know would never choose to drive anywhere on a snow-covered road."

She chuckled softly. "I discovered tonight that with God's help I can handle what comes my way." She shrugged. "And if two little puppies that I adore need rescuing..."

He saw a hint of fear in her eyes, but knew she'd do it for him. "How about you call Josh?"

She nodded and left the room.

His heart swelled with love for this woman who'd overcome her deepest fear to help him. The door opened a moment later and Keira came in. Her face was flushed and her hands shook. "What's wrong?"

"Nothing. When I couldn't reach Josh I called Susan.

Apparently they went to his in-law's house for Christmas. They left early this morning."

"That settles it." He sat up, slower this time. "I'm going home. And I'm driving myself." His firm tone left no room for argument. No matter how much Keira claimed she was okay to drive, he knew otherwise. "You look ready to faint with the thought of driving back to my place."

"But I said I would. Besides, you can't drive. The doctor said—"

"I know." His shoulders slumped. "Any chance you could stay on the couch at my place tonight?"

"I don't think so." Keira's eyes widened. "What about a neighbor? Couldn't you get someone to let the dogs out and then feed them in the morning?"

That might work. He'd left the house unlocked. "Don't know why I didn't think of that."

"Probably the pounding headache you're pretending doesn't exist." Keira scowled.

He motioned to the bag on the bedside table. "My phone's in there."

She pulled it out and handed it to him.

Although he lived in the country, he still had neighbors within walking distance. Thankfully the woman up the road answered. He explained the situation and she agreed to take care of the dogs once he assured her they were friendly puppies.

He closed the phone. "Thanks for the suggestion. I hate to bother people with stuff like that, but sometimes it can't be helped."

Keira yawned and stood. "You going to stay put and be a good patient now?"

"I'll try." He reached out and took her hand again. "Thanks for rescuing me."

She blushed. "Don't mention it. What about your knee? You never said."

"Just a sprain. It'll take time to heal. In the meantime there's no skiing for me."

"Bummer. It was kind of fun until you crashed." She took a step away from him, forcing him to release her hand. "I should get home. I work in the morning."

"Christmas Eve. I'll bet Cody will be wired all day."

"Probably. He'll spend most of the day with his grandparents. They'll bring him home at two when I lock up."

"I'm glad you're closing early. Will you be attending the Living Nativity?"

"Always. It's tradition. A group of us walk to the church together. If you're up to it, you're welcome to join us."

"Thanks, but I don't think walking will work for me this year." Although he would like nothing better. If he wanted his knee to heal he shouldn't tire it the day after injuring it.

"I understand, but maybe I'll see you there."

"Okay." He didn't want Keira to leave, but couldn't think of another reason to keep her by his side any longer.

She wiggled her fingers at him and walked out of the

room.

Loneliness filled the void her absence left. He longed for her company.

A few minutes later the door whooshed open again, startling him from his thoughts. Keira poked her head in. "Tell you what. My apartment is close and quite comfy. If you'd like. I'll watch over you until you're out of the woods. I've decided to stay up and bake Christmas cookies all night just to make sure you're okay."

"Yes!"

She laughed. "I'll wait outside while you get dressed. I already talked with your doctor, and he said if you agreed it'd be fine."

Pete changed as quickly as his throbbing head allowed, then hobbled to the door. He stepped into the hall and spotted Keira talking with the doctor. Trying hard not to limp, he approached them.

The doctor shook his hand. "Looks like you're free after all. If you have any problems, give me a call, and don't forget to schedule a follow-up visit with your personal physician."

"Thanks for everything. Doc."

Keira grinned, but a worried look haunted her eyes.

She spun around and marched toward the door, then called over her shoulder, "I'll bring your rig up to the door. Wait for me."

Keira handed Pete an armload of blankets and the pillow

from her son's bed. "I'd offer you Cody's bed but it's toddler-size and half your body would hang over the end."

"No worries. The couch is fine."

"Well, it's comfortable at least." She looked around the small apartment for anything that needed tending, but everything looked tidy. "I'll wake you in a couple hours so you don't sleep too deeply and never wake up."

"You don't need to do that. I'll be fine."

"I promised the doctor I would, and I keep my word. Sweet dreams." She headed to the kitchen.

"Will you keep me company for a while first?"

She quirked a brow.

He chuckled and winced. "Oh, that was a bad idea. Sorry I asked."

She walked over to the chaise, dropped into it and curled her feet under her. "No, it's fine. I'll sit with you for a little while. I have the rest of the night to bake cookies and watch Christmas movies."

"Do you ever have trouble sleeping?"

"Occasionally." She hadn't had many restful nights since Cody was born, and the past couple had been filled with thoughts of Pete, but he didn't need to know that.

"I'm usually out like a rock within minutes, but something tells me I'll be awake tonight."

"At least you're not vomiting from your concussion. That happened to someone I knew."

He winced again. "Guess I'm lucky."

"Are you warm enough?"

"Toasty. Thanks for the sweats and T-shirt."

"You're welcome. The T-shirt is a little snug, but I'm afraid that's the best I can do." Actually it was a lot snug. Pete had biceps Michael had only dreamed of having.

She'd never been able to part with Michael's favorite sweatpants and T-shirt—had even worn them herself from time to time over the past few years. Granted they swam on her, but on those lonely nights they were a comfort.

Keira stumbled around for something to talk about and drew a blank. What she really needed was sleep, but she wanted to be sure he was okay. She often had to stay up with Cody when he didn't feel well. Must be a male trait because when she didn't feel well, she wanted to be left alone.

"What's the smirk about?"

She jumped. "I don't know what you're talking about." She couldn't stop the grin that spread across her face. Standing, she flipped off the main lights and plugged in the Christmas tree.

"What's wrong, Keira? Don't want me to see your face?"

She wagged her finger at him and flashed a grin. "You'd better behave or I'll send you back to the medical center. You can sleep in the waiting room."

He held up his hands. "No, not that. I'll be good." He rested his head back and his eyes drooped.

Keira giggled, then sobered. The man had fallen asleep. Guess he was more tired than he'd let on. She stood and padded to the kitchen and turned on the oven.

"What do you mean, he spent the night!" Susan shouted into the phone.

Keira pulled the phone away from her ear until her friend became quiet. "What are you shouting about? You make it sound like we did something wrong. He slept on the couch while I baked cookies in the kitchen and sat up and watched movies in the living room." Irritation laced her voice.

"You can't just bring a man to your home, Keira."

"What did you expect me to do? He has a concussion and needed someone to keep an eye on him. I figured it was better to let him use my couch than have him sneak home in the wee hours of the morning and possibly kill himself along the way."

"Not everyone dies in car crashes. It's been four years. When are you going to get over it?"

Keira sucked in her breath and her throat burned. "I have to go." She swallowed back the tears. "Catch you later."

"Don't hang up. I was out of line." Susan's voice softened. "I'm sorry. I Just freaked because I don't want you to be the object of gossip. Please don't be angry."

"It's fine. Really, I have a lot to do this morning before work." She pushed End, tossed the phone on the bed beside her and wrapped her arms around her middle. She knew her friend was right and didn't mean to hurt her, but it was so hard to not be afraid of what-ifs. Closing her eyes, she fought the threatening tears but lost the battle. A sob escaped. Her shoulders shook.

Susan just didn't understand. She couldn't. She'd never lost someone in an accident. She didn't know what it was like to wonder every time someone she loved walked out the door if they would come back. Susan didn't know the fear in her gut when Cody left with his grandparents. Or the knot in her stomach when the phone rang or someone knocked on the door unexpectedly, just like the night her husband had been killed. For months after his death she'd dreaded answering the phone or the door.

Sure, she'd made great progress and rarely freaked out when the phone rang now, but the fear always hovered in the deep recesses of her mind.

A knock on her bedroom door caused her to jump. She cleared her throat. "Yes?"

"Everything okay?" Pete asked.

"Fine. I'll be out soon." Keira wiped her eyes and took several calming breaths. She was glad her friend didn't know any of those feelings. But Susan was right, she needed to stop expecting the worst. God had helped her last night. He'd been with her every minute she was behind the wheel. She would trust him with her future, with Cody, and even with Pete.

It was time to start living and put the fear behind her. She looked at the closed door, hoping her future waited on the other side. Because last night had proved without a doubt she loved Pete.

Pete sat on the couch and stared at Keira's closed bedroom door. He'd heard her crying a moment ago and heard the thickness of her voice when she'd replied. He wanted to comfort her, but clearly she wanted to be left alone. He'd respect her privacy.

The door swung open a few minutes later and she stepped out. "Good morning. How's your head today?"

"Not too bad, at least the headache's gone." He stood and followed her to the kitchen. "I started the coffee. I hope that's okay."

"Better than. Thanks." She took a mug from the cupboard. Filled it half-full with milk and creamer, then added coffee. She took a sip and made a face.

"You don't like it?"

"It's just a little stronger than I'm used to."

"I don't know how you can taste it with all that milk and cream."

She shrugged.

He set his mug on the counter. "How about you let me treat you to breakfast?" He'd changed into his now-dry clothes and managed to at least look almost put together. "The coffee shop?"

"Sure. Seems to be our place."

She giggled and poured the coffee down the drain, then clicked off the coffeemaker. "Let's go." She grabbed her coat, purse and keys and headed for the door that led down to the candy shop.

He followed. "What's your hurry?"

She slowed. "Sorry. I forgot about your knee."

He reached out for her hand and stopped her before they exited the shop. "In case I forgot to say it, thanks for rescuing me last night."

She ducked her head. "You already thanked me."

He tilted her chin up with his finger and her sea-green eyes slammed into his. "You are an amazing woman, Keira." He lowered his mouth to hers and placed a gentle kiss on her soft lips.

She ran her thumb along the top of his hand and studied his face. "May I ask you something?"

He nodded.

"What are we doing?"

He ran his fingers through her hair. "I thought we were going for coffee." He grinned, then sobered when she didn't smile. "I know some people take kissing lightly, but I don't. I really care about you, Keira."

Her lips formed a soft O, and he read a mixture of fear and excitement in her eyes.

"I hope you feel the same way."

She nodded shyly.

He loved this woman, but didn't want to scare her away by saying so too soon. Then again, hadn't she said she loved him when she thought he was unconscious? He still wasn't sure if he'd imagined that. No, he'd wait a little longer, just to be safe.

"Do you think we could get breakfast now? I have several orders to prepare before I open at ten."

He tugged her toward the exit. "Let's go get a caffeine fix and some food." Good thing he'd already called in sick, because he had the sudden urge to visit the jewelry store.

14

Keira stood behind the candy counter shortly before closing on Christmas Eve, waiting for the last customer to finish making her selections. She marveled at how some people waited to shop until the last minute. This woman couldn't have cut it any closer. The store closed in ten minutes.

The door opened and Susan rushed in. "I made it! Quick, I forgot to get my best client a gift. Do you have any more of those raspberry-ganache-filled dark chocolates? I know he'll love them."

"A few." Keira fingered the serving tongs she used. "What size box?"

"The small round one."

"Okay. Would you like an assortment of dark chocolates to finish it off?"

"Sure. Just make it fast. He's going to be at my office in five minutes."

"I didn't know you gave clients gifts." Keira made quick work of putting the gift together and handed it to her friend. "It's on me."

"I'd argue, but don't have time." She grabbed the candy and strode for the door. "Are we still walking to the Living Nativity together tonight?"

"Yes, and come early. I have some stuff to tell you." She couldn't stop the smile that covered her face.

"Okay. Our conversation this morning did leave a lot unsaid. See you later."

Keira frowned. She'd nearly forgotten about Susan's outburst regarding Pete staying on her couch. What she really wanted to tell her was about the man himself and how things were progressing between them.

The woman who'd been filling up bags from the bins finally approached the counter. "I think that will do it. I have four kids, and I don't want any of them to feel cheated." Four kids with a sugar high on Christmas? Keira held back a shudder. Even though she owned a candy shop, Cody rarely ate any and she never gave him sweets for Christmas. Instead she loaded him up with healthier choices. Although she had to admit as he got older that was becoming more of a challenge.

She finished ringing up the sale and walked the woman to the door. "Have a merry Christmas."

"Thanks." The woman rushed away. She probably still needed to pick up other presents, too. Keira chuckled and locked up, thankful her own shopping was complete as well as her contribution to Christmas dinner—frozen veggies that only needed to be microwaved. It didn't get easier than that. Plus she had those dozens of Christmas cookies she'd baked last night.

She went into the storage room and found Cody watching *Frosty the Snowman* for probably the third time this year. "Hey there. You ready to head upstairs?"

Cody hopped off his cot and closed the portable DVD player. "Yep." He took her hand and they climbed the stairs together. "What are we going to do now, Momma?"

"I don't know." A nap sounded nice. On top of staying up all night baking, she'd been going nonstop since she'd opened. "Did you have something in mind?"

"I was hoping to play with Max and Molly today."

"Oh, I don't think so. Mr. Pete injured himself while we were skiing. and I imagine he's not up to visiting."

Cody's bottom lip protruded. "Can't we call him? Please?" He dragged out the word in a whiney voice.

Keira sighed. She knew how much her son wanted to see the dogs, but didn't want to spoil his Christmas surprise, either. "Sorry, buddy. How about a game, or we could play in the snow?"

Cody gave a halfhearted shrug and shuffled to the back door. "Let's play in the snow." He slid into his boots. "It won't be as fun without Max and Molly, though."

Just wait, little one. Keira kept a straight face and readied herself for the outdoors. Her insides were dancing just thinking about how surprised her son would be in the morning. This would definitely be the best Christmas ever.

Keira explained in a whisper to Susan about last

night. To her friend's credit she didn't say a word as they strolled toward their church to watch the outdoor Living Nativity. She went on to tell her that things had changed between her and Pete, and she felt like they had a future together.

"Do you think he'll propose soon?" Susan asked, wide-eyed.

"Of course not. It's too soon. We've only known each other a little over two months."

Susan waved a hand at her. "That's not important." She patted her chest. "It's what's in here that matters. If you love him and he loves you, then that's all that's important." A sad smile touched her lips. "At least that's all that should matter."

Keira pursed her lips, suspecting Susan was thinking about her broken engagement several years ago. "Well, I don't know if Pete loves me. Although I think he might." A small smile turned up the corners of her lips. "He sure kisses like he does."

Susan squealed. "He kissed you!"

"Sush." She looked around to see if anyone had heard, but no one was paying any attention except Cody.

He looked up at her. "Who kissed you, Momma?" Susan mouthed *sorry*.

Keira didn't want to lie to her son, but at the same time wasn't sure how he'd take what she had to say. She didn't want to confuse him or raise false hope, either. However she refused to be anything but truthful and decided just laying it out there would be best. "Mr. Pete."

"Does that mean he's going to be my dad now?"

Her mind slipped back to several weeks ago when Cody had asked the same question, only this time she *really* didn't know how to answer him. "Would you like that?" He nodded with a cheesy grin.

Keira's stomach flip-flopped at the idea, but she was being silly. She refused to give the idea another thought. At least for now.

Pete spotted Keira, Cody and Susan as they walked toward the church and the crowd that gathered outside. He waved and smiled when Keira noticed him. The trio approached him a minute later.

"You made it." Keira stood on tiptoe and planted a kiss on his cheek. "How're you feeling?"

"Not too bad. How was your day?" He loved the feel of his hand against the small of her back.

"Busy to start, but Cody and I had a nice afternoon playing in the snow. Then I made spaghetti for dinner."

He ruffled Cody's hair. "Sounds like you had a fun day."

Cody nodded, then motioned with his finger for him to come down to his level. Easier said than done with his knee feeling the way it was, but he muscled through the pain and squatted beside the child. "What's up?"

"Are you going to marry my mom?" Cody whispered.

Pete rocked back on his heels and landed on his bottom.

"You okay?" Keira asked.

"Fine." At least physically. He rolled over onto all fours and whispered into Cody's ear before standing. A huge grin covered Cody's face. Pete touched a finger to his lips.

"What was that all about?" Keira kept her voice low as the presentation began.

"Man stuff." He wrapped an arm around her shoulders, tugged her close and turned his attention to the nativity as the narrator started talking. He rubbed his palm up and down her arm to help ward off the chill. The outdoor performance drew him in, and he soon forgot about the cold.

Pete had an inkling of the love Joseph must have felt for Mary. Hopefully his situation would turn out as well as Joseph's. One thing he did know for certain, he loved Keira and her son and wanted to spend the rest of his life with them.

Early Christmas morning, before the sun was even shining, Keira heard a tap at her apartment door. A moment later she opened the door and touched a finger to her lips. "Come in, Pete." She stepped aside, allowing him to pass with the dog crate that seemed to hold all the supplies he'd picked up for Max. "Cody's still sleeping, but he'll wake up soon. How're you feeling? Do you need any help?"

"No, thanks. I'm fine." He placed a quick kiss on her forehead. "I'll be right back with Max."

Keira quickly arranged a doggie bed and a basket

filled with doggie treats near the Christmas tree, where a few other gifts were waiting to be opened. The door opened and Pete limped in carrying Max, who wore a red handkerchief around his neck, from which a tag hung that said Merry Christmas.

"What do you think?" Pete held up the wiggling dog.

"He's perfect. Quick. Go put him by the tree. I hear Cody rustling around in his room." She plugged in the tree lights and turned off all the others. Soft Christmas music filled the room.

Cody walked in, rubbing his eyes.

Keira flipped on the light. "Merry Christmas!"

Cody blinked and looked toward the tree. He caught his breath when he spotted Pete holding Max. A huge smile covered Cody's face. "Mr. Pete, you came!" He ran at Pete and tackled his legs with a hug.

Pete grunted and held Max higher to protect him from the rambunctious preschooler. "Yep, and your mom has a little surprise for you, too." He lowered the puppy and handed him to Cody.

Cody's eyes widened and his gaze shot to Keira. "For me?"

"Max is your Christmas present." She smiled wide.

"No way!" Laughter burst from his lips. He hugged Max close. "I love you, Max. Thanks, Mom."

"I think he liked your surprise," Pete whispered beside her.

"Mm-hmm." Keira swiped tears from her eyes, laughing at her overemotional response. She took Pete's hand and held it tight. "Thanks for making this happen. This is the best Christmas ever. I've never seen my son so happy."

"You're welcome. Thanks for inviting me to be a part of it." Pete withdrew his hand and sat on the floor in front of the tree. "What do you say we see what else you got?"

Cody leaped toward the gifts.

"Hold on just one minute." Keira sat next to Pete. "Why don't you let Mr. Pete hand you your gifts, rather than go into attack mode?"

Pete handed Cody a package Keira didn't recognize. He ripped off the wrap and jumped up and down. "My own camera!"

"I thought you'd enjoy taking pictures of Max."

"Thanks, Mr. Pete!"

"You're welcome." A warm smile touched his lips and he looked as if he belonged in their living room. He handed another gift to her son.

Cody finished opening presents, then moved on to his stocking. "This is the best Christmas ever." He flung himself into Keira's arms. "Thanks, Mom. I wanted more Hot Wheels."

"You're welcome." She leaned against the couch and ran her fingers thorough his hair. He looked so much like his dad, but she saw some of herself in him, too. "Would you like pancakes for breakfast?"

"Yum. With gummy worms."

"Eww!" Pete's lips curled. "That's disgusting."

"No, it's not," Cody said. "They look really cool coming out of the whipped cream."

"Oh. There's whipped cream? That changes everything."

Keira laughed and pushed up. "Why don't you take Mr. Pete down to the store and have him help you pick out a few from the bin."

She shook her head and looked at Pete. "I forgot about your knee. I'll take him down."

"I'm much better. We'll be right back."

"If you're sure."

"Positive."

She knelt in front of her son. "Remember, a few is three—no more."

"Okay. Thanks!" He tugged on Pete's hand. "Come on."

Keira turned on the griddle, then stirred water into the store mix until the consistency looked right. Footsteps clopped on the stairs.

Cody pushed through the door, then dropped the candy on the kitchen counter. "Here, Mom. I only took three."

"Good job. Go play, and I'll call you when breakfast is ready." She'd set the table the night before, to simplify things.

"What can I do to help?" Pete stood at the opening to the kitchen, rubbing his hands together as if he were anxious to get to work.

"Would you like to finish up the pancakes, and I'll pour the coffee?"

"Sure." He brushed up next to her, invading her space and trapping her.

Keira's face warmed, and she tried to move away, but there was nowhere to go in the tiny kitchen.

Meanwhile he went about flipping pancakes with a tiny grin on his face.

"I suppose you find this funny." She crossed her arms.

"I don't know what you're talking about." He moved the cooked food to a platter. "Would you keep these warm in the oven, please?"

Keira took the platter and slid it into the oven.

"Mom, can Max play in my room?"

"Only if all your toys are picked up."

"They are." He wrinkled his brow. "Mr. Pete, where's Molly?"

"At home. She's fine for a couple hours by herself."

"Oh. Isn't she lonely?"

Keira stepped between them. "If you want to play you'd better get moving. Breakfast will be ready very soon."

"Okay." Cody clapped his hands, and Max followed him.

Pete's attention had shifted to her. "Thanks for the save. He's a good kid. Anyone would be proud to call him son."

"Thanks." She looked up at him. Was he trying to tell

her something? His gaze locked with hers, knocking her train of thought right out the window and into the next county. "I mean..." She shook her head. "Never mind." There'd be plenty of time to have this conversation—after coffee.

His eyes sparkled. "You sure? Seems like you have something important on your mind."

"Nothing that won't keep. Looks like we have plenty of pancakes. I'll grab the syrup if you want to set the platter on the table." Keira squeezed past him and grabbed the syrup from the cupboard, then hollered for Cody to wash his hands. She set it down, then spun to get the coffee, but Pete had beat her to it.

"Should I leave room for cream?" He waggled his brows.

"Only fill it half-full. I like a lot of milk in mine and a generous amount of creamer."

"I was teasing. Who could forget you're one of those people who like a little coffee with their cream?" He handed her the half-full cup.

"It's pretty good. You should try it." She filled the rest with milk and cream, then held the mug out to him.

He took a sip and made a face. "Too sweet. But I suppose you're full of sugar and spice and everything nice." He winked and moved to the table.

They sat and Pete opened his hands to Keira and Cody. Keira grasped it and Cody followed her example.

Pete closed his eyes and prayed over their meal, then gave her hand a gentle squeeze and let go. "This looks delicious."

"Mom, where's the whipped cream and gummy worms?"

Keira jumped up. "I forgot. Just a second." She went into the kitchen, pulled the can from the fridge, swiped the candy from the counter and created her son's favorite breakfast. "How's that?"

"Yum!" Cody pulled a gummy worm from the center of the whipped cream and sucked off the cream. "Thanks, Mom."

She smiled and tried to ignore Pete's horrified look. Guess he didn't have the taste buds of a four-year-old.

Pete chuckled. The child would be on a sugar high for hours. Of course, so would Keira, with all the sweet creamer she'd used.

"Grandma said we could go sledding when we get to her house."

"Sounds like fun." Pete picked up his coffee and brought it to his lips. The warmth spread through his chest. Keira might not be much of a cook, but she could brew an amazing cup of coffee.

"You know, if you change your mind you're welcome to join us for the entire day," Keira said.

"Thanks, but I don't think so." Spending the day with Keira and Cody, appealed, but he didn't want to intrude on their family. He really wanted some time alone with her, but the chances of that happening were probably slim.

Cody patted his stomach. "I'm full. Can I play now?"

"Sure. Put your dishes on the counter, and wash your hands. I don't want Max covered in syrup."

Pete grinned. "He'd probably lick Cody clean before that could happen."

She shook her head and stood. "If you're finished I'll take your plate and load the dishwasher."

He handed his dish over, deciding it'd be best not to invade her space again but instead pushed back from the table and brought his coffee to the bar. Cody had disappeared into his bedroom. "I'm not working tomorrow. Any chance you'd be free for coffee or something?"

"You mean like a date?" Her hands stopped midair and she held a drippy plate over the sink.

"Yeah." He cleared his throat.

The hint of a smile touched her lips and she set the plate in the dishwasher. "Go on."

"When I first came to Leavenworth the furthest thing from my mind was finding someone like you. Then there you were, and I freaked because of your son. I'm so sorry for that. I want a relationship with you and Cody."

A full-fledged smile broke across her face. "He got to you, huh?"

"Yeah." Pete pushed back from the counter. "So did his mom." He sauntered into the kitchen, not caring anymore if he invaded her space. He had every intention of doing just that.

Her eyes widened and she caught her breath.

In two strides she was within the circle of his arms. He reached around her and shut off the water. He lowered his mouth to hers and probed her soft lips. She responded hesitantly at first, then her hands slid up his chest and cradled his neck. "I love you, Keira."

She looked at him with wide eyes. "I love you, too."

He buried his face in her neck and breathed in the scent of her clean skin. "You smell good."

She gently pushed him away and distanced herself from his touch. He wanted to reach out and pull her to him again, but noticed the wary look in her eyes. What had he done wrong? It was only a kiss. "Is everything okay?"

"Of course. I just don't want to get carried away." Her cheeks matched the color of the red berries tucked into the Christmas tree. "And I don't want to move too fast."

"Was that too fast?" It wasn't like it was the first time they'd kissed.

"Like a speeding train." She wrapped her arms around her middle. "I haven't been kissed like that since...I can't remember."

Pleased by her statement, he stood just a bit straighter. "There's more where that came from." He winked.

She giggled. "You're missing the point."

He sobered. "No, I hear you. I'm only teasing." He reached for her hand and drew her back to him. "I never thought I could feel this way about anyone."

"Especially someone with a child?" She raised a brow. He groaned. "Can we forget I ever said I don't date women with children?"

She cradled his face in her hands. "Don't give it another thought. I love you even more for your honesty." She planted a kiss on his cheek and moved away. "You sure you won't spend the day with us?"

Tempted to say yes, he hesitated. "I really want to, but I feel weird about intruding on Michael's parents. After all, I'm extremely interested in their daughter-in-law and, well..." He rubbed the back of his neck. "It just feels awkward. After all, you were married to their son."

"I want you to come with us today. Mary already thinks the world of you."

He worked his jaw. "But she doesn't know me."

"Doesn't matter. Apparently Cody has given her all the important details. Please come. You'll save me from having to drive." She raised her brows as if saving her was an enticing offer. Who was he kidding? He'd do anything for her.

15

Keira clasped her hands tightly together in the passenger seat and peered out the windshield. Cody sat with Max behind her in his booster seat, singing "Frosty the Snowman." Why did he have to sing *that* song? As if she needed reminding that it was snowing.

"How're you doing?" Pete glanced in her direction. "You look like you might be sick."

"No, I'm fine, but it's still hard riding in a car."

"You're doing a great job. I'm proud of you."

"Me, too, Momma." Cody stopped singing long enough to join in the conversation. "Grandma and Grandpa will be so surprised. Won't they, Mom?"

"About what?"

"Grandma said they came to our place last year because of the snow."

"Oh. That's right." She'd forgotten. In fact she'd managed to get out of Christmas at her in-laws' since Michael's death. Funny that hadn't occurred to her until Cody brought it up.

Pete pulled into their driveway and parked. "Would you like help carrying things in before I take off to get Molly?"

"No, thanks." She raised the box filled with gifts and dog supplies. "I got it, and Cody can be responsible for Max."

Pete glanced toward the house. "They know I'm coming, right?"

"Yes, and they're thrilled."

"I wish I had gifts for them. I could probably dig something up from home, though, when I pick up Molly."

She rested her hand on his. "They don't expect anything, but if it will make you feel better, I'll add your name to our gifts."

"No." He shook his head. "You're right. It's not a big deal."

Cody stood between the seats. "Can we go in now? Grandma said she has a special surprise for me."

Keira laughed. "Make sure Max is on his leash."

"I did." He moved to get out and stopped. "Mr. Pete?"

"Yeah, buddy?"

"I'm glad you're here."

"Thanks. Hop on out, and I'll go pick up Molly and be back before you know it."

Cody opened the door and jumped out. "Come on. Max." He patted his thighs and the dog scrambled down.

"You'll drive carefully, right?" Keira couldn't help the unease in her stomach. It was a day much like today that

Michael had lost control on that turn.

"I promise." He leaned over and placed a soft kiss on her lips.

Keira nearly floated into the house, her face heated at the knowing look on Mary's face. "Merry Christmas! Where's Pete going?"

"To get his puppy. He hadn't planned on coming with us, and she's too young to stay locked up all day at his place." Cody held up Max for his grandma to see. "Isn't he the best?"

Mary took the puppy and snuggled him close. "Absolutely. That was sure nice of your momma to get you a dog for Christmas. Are you going to take him for walks and feed him and clean up after him?"

Cody cast a worried look toward Keira.

"Don't worry, sweetie. We'll do it together."

Mary pulled her into the kitchen. "How do you plan to take care of a puppy, your son and the store all at the same time?"

She stifled a sigh. Mary was practical to a fault. She couldn't even give them one day to enjoy Christmas without pointing out the challenges of pet ownership. Oh, well. She refused to let it spoil the day. "It's all taken care of. I'm only working five days a week now, and I hired a dog walker to take Max out on the days I work."

Mary grinned. "I'm proud of you, Keira. You've really grown a lot over the past month or so. I never thought I'd see the day you'd relinquish your store to the care of anyone, much less get a puppy." She pulled a cake

211

from the oven. "On top of that, you came to *us* this Christmas." She placed the cake on the counter. "We are so pleased at your progress."

Keira swallowed the lump in her throat. "Thanks. May I ask you something?"

"Of course."

"Are you okay with Pete coming here today?"

"We couldn't be happier. Seems to me he's a big reason for the changes we've seen in you."

"I suppose he has a lot to do with it, but it was time, and God's been working on me."

Mary pulled her into a warm hug. "Amen." She dabbed her watery eyes. "How long till that man of yours returns?"

"He's not my man." Well, then again, maybe he was.

"If you say so, but my eyes don't lie. I saw him kiss you before he left. Should we do the tree without him or wait?"

"I don't think it matters. He was concerned about not having a gift for you and Dad."

She waved a hand. "No problem, but I think we should exchange gifts now if you think that would make him more comfortable. And if he shows up in the middle, then no biggie."

"That's a great idea. Cody's pretty excited. I'm not sure you'd be able to keep him from snooping."

Mary laughed and linked arms with her as they strolled into the family room, where Cody sat on his grandpa's knee, bouncing up and down. When he spotted

212

them he hopped off and ran to Mary, wrapping his little arms around her legs. "Can we open presents now?"

"You bet."

Keira took Cody's hand and guided him to the couch. A short time later Cody tore into his first present, and not long afterward paper was strewn around the room. Cody held a large bag filled to overflowing with watercolor paint, modeling clay, coloring and activity books, sketch pads, crayons and more—all things he could play with quietly in the storage room while she worked. They'd even included a few DVDs.

Keira still needed to open her gift since she'd been watching everyone open their gifts. Finally she tore away the wrap on a smallish box just as the doorbell pealed.

"Mr. Pete!" Cody sprang up and ran to the door.

Keira was torn between the gift and Pete.

"Well, what do you think?" Mary asked.

"I love it. I've always wanted a digital picture frame."

Pete came into the room, being dragged by Cody. He held Molly and what looked like a loaf of bread wrapped in foil. "Merry Christmas, everyone."

Keira stood and walked over to him. She scratched Molly's back. "Max is on his bed." She motioned toward the fireplace.

"He looks content."

"Yeah, I think he's enjoying the heat from the fire." Pete set Molly beside her brother, and the puppies rustled around a little before settling down for another nap.

Keira yawned and stretched, then plopped down

onto the couch. "I need more caffeine."

"I brought cranberry bread. Should I put it in the kitchen?"

Mary rose and took the loaf. "That was nice of you. Keira didn't mention you bake."

He sat beside Keira and rested his arm behind her on the back of the couch. "I'm not sure she knew."

"Pete is full of culinary surprises."

"Oh, I'm full of more than just culinary surprises."

Keira's brows lifted. Sounded like Pete might be up to something. Her pulse quickened.

Pete needed some air. The sun was setting and the package in his pocket was driving him to distraction. "Keira, would you like to take a walk?"

"What about your knee?"

"It only hurts a little."

Uncertainty covered her face.

"Please." He lowered his voice. "I need to get a little fresh air."

She glanced at Cody, who played a game with his grandpa. "I suppose it'll be okay since Mary's taking a nap anyway. Can't say I blame her. That meal was amazing. She must have been cooking for days."

Pete slipped on his boots and shrugged into his jacket. He held Keira's for her as she slid her arms in.

She looked over her shoulder and grinned. "Thanks."

Oh, how he wanted to kiss her again. "Ready?

"Shouldn't we take the dogs?"

"Probably. But let's not." He wanted Keira's undivided attention and those dogs guaranteed a distraction.

"We won't be long," Keira called out to her father-in-law.

He waved them off. "Enjoy your walk."

Keira stepped out the door in front of Pete and waited on the stoop. He took her hand and they walked to the edge of the driveway and stopped. The road had been plowed, but probably wouldn't be the safest place to walk. He turned around and took in the yard for the first time. He spotted a bench swing hanging from an oversized arbor covered in tiny white lights near a huge tree. There was actually a tall portable propane heater next to it. It looked like Keira's in-laws enjoyed that spot frequently.

An idea quickly formed in his mind and he couldn't wipe the smile from his face. This was it. He guided her back to his 4Runner, where he grabbed a couple blankets.

"What are you doing?" Keira looked at him like he'd lost his mind.

"I thought we could sit on that swing." He handed her the blankets and moved over to brush it clear of snow. "See."

"Now all we need is a bonfire to keep us warm."

He turned on the heater and took the blankets from her arms. "That's what these are for." They each wrapped up in one and sat shoulder to shoulder.

"Mmm. That heater feels good." Keira rested her

head against his shoulder.

"Today was nice. Your in-laws were gracious hosts."

"Thanks. Cody loves his grandparents. Especially his grandpa. He's sort of a surrogate father to him."

Pete fingered the box in his pocket. He knew without a doubt he loved Keira and her son. They'd become a part of his life and he couldn't imagine not being with them.

Keira gently moved the swing back and forth with her feet, the squeak of the chain the only sound in the still air. It had stopped snowing hours ago. The fresh blanket of snow muffled any other noises.

Keira nudged his shoulder. "You're so quiet. Something on your mind?"

"A lot, actually." He hesitated. Was it too soon? Even if it was, he had to take the chance. Life was too short to wait. He dropped to one knee in front of Keira.

She caught her breath. "What are you doing? You'll get wet. And what about your knee?"

He took her hands and cradled them in his. "Stop worrying. I'm fine, but I have something I want to say."

She nodded, her eyes filled with wonder. Or was it fear? Or maybe it was love.

"My life changed the day I walked into your shop to buy a box of chocolates for our blind date. You changed me." He chuckled. "You and Cody. What a pair you are. Your son has more energy than I imagined possible and more love than I've ever hoped for. Together the two of you complete me. Things I believed about myself turned out to be false, and thanks to you I realized it. You helped me see past the hurt from a broken relationship and gave me the courage to trust again." He pulled the box from his pocket. "I want to be your husband."

He opened the lid, exposing the princess-cut diamond ring. "Keira, I love you with all my heart. Will you marry me?"

Keira's eyes glistened and she nodded. She held out her shaking hand.

He tugged her glove off and slipped the ring on her finger. "A perfect fit."

Keira gazed at the ring for a moment and then at the man who'd changed her life. Every nerve ending in her body tingled and she wanted to dance. With her heart full to overflowing, she stood, drawing him up with her. "I never dreamed I'd love anyone like this again. I love you so much and so does Cody." She wrapped her arms around his neck. "Talk about a surprise. Thanks for making this the best Christmas ever." She placed a gentle kiss on his lips and nuzzled into the crook of his neck.

A tug on her jacket made her jump. She looked down. "Cody! What are you doing out here?"

"Is Mr. Pete going to be my dad now?"

Pete chuckled and hoisted her son into his arms. "Not today, buddy. I think your mom and I need a little time to enjoy being engaged."

Keira looked toward the house and spotted her in-laws standing in the doorway, wearing wide grins. "Did they know?"

Pete shook his head. "I didn't say anything."

"I told them you had a little box in your hand and Grandpa hollered for Grandma. We watched from the window." Cody reached for her hand and studied her ring. "It sparkles." He patted Pete's shoulder. "Good job, Mr. Pete."

Keira laughed and drew her men close. "Yes, but I'd call it a great job!"

~The End~

Author Note

Dear Reader,

Thank you for reading A Christmas Promise. I hope you enjoyed Keira's story of overcoming her fear and finding love again.

I knew I wanted to set my story in Leavenworth, Washington because I couldn't imagine a more Christmasy town. I asked my mom to come with me on a research trip and together we road Amtrak to the quaint Bavarian Village in the Cascades. Our visit there was made all the more sweeter because my husband's extended family live there, and they took us around the town to show us all sorts of sites. I was also able to interview them over breakfast one morning and get a feel for the people there. It was a really special experience and one I will always treasure.

The next book in Love Stories from Leavenworth, Washington will release next moth.

You can contact me via my website www.kimberlyrjohnson.com as well as sign up for my newsletter.

Blessings,
Kimberly Rose Johnson

Books by
Kimberly Rose Johnson

Melodies of Love
A Love Song for Kayla
An Encore for Estelle
A Waltz for Amber (Coming soon!)

Sunriver Dreams
A Love to Treasure
A Christmas Homecoming
Designing Love

Wildflower B&B Romance Series
Island Refuge
Island Dreams
Island Christmas
Island Hope

Contemporary Inspirational Romance Collection
In Love and War

Stand-alone novella
Brewed with Love

Love in the Cascades
A Christmas Surprise
A Rekindled Romance
A Love that Lasts
The Matchmaker's Match